THE BEST WORST SUMMER

Also by Elizabeth Eulberg:

THE BEST WORST SUMMER

ELIZABETH EULBERG

BLOOMSBURY
CHILDREN'S BOOKS
NEW YORK LONDON OXFORD NEW DELHI SYDNEY

BLOOMSBURY CHILDREN'S BOOKS
Bloomsbury Publishing Inc., part of Bloomsbury Publishing Plc
1385 Broadway, New York, NY 10018

BLOOMSBURY, BLOOMSBURY CHILDREN'S BOOKS, and the Diana logo
are trademarks of Bloomsbury Publishing Plc

First published in the United States of America in May 2021
by Bloomsbury Children's Books

Bloomsbury books may be purchased for business or promotional use.
For information on bulk purchases please contact
Macmillan Corporate and Premium Sales Department at specialmarkets@macmillan.com

Library of Congress Cataloging-in-Publication Data
Names: Eulberg, Elizabeth, author.
Title: The best worst summer / by Elizabeth Eulberg.
Description: New York : Bloomsbury Children's Books, 2021.
Summary: Peyton, who is having the worst summer ever after moving away from her best friend, finds a
box buried in her back yard while, in 1989, Mel and Jess embark on their best summer.
Identifiers: LCCN 2020053966 (print) | LCCN 2020053967 (e-book)
ISBN 9781547601509 (hardcover) • ISBN 9781547601516 (e-book)
Subjects: CYAC: Best friends—Fiction. | Friendship—Fiction. | Moving, Household—Fiction. |
Family life—Fiction.
Classification: LCC PZ7.E8685 Ber 2021 (print) | LCC PZ7.E8685 (e-book) | DDC [Fic]—dc23
LC record available at https://lccn.loc.gov/2020053966

Book design by Jeanette Levy
Typeset by Westchester Publishing Services
Printed and bound in the U.S.A. by Berryville Graphics Inc., Berryville, Virginia
2 4 6 8 10 9 7 5 3 1

To find out more about our authors and books visit
www.bloomsbury.com and sign up for our newsletters.

For Tara—who spent all those summers going to Book World and eating cheeseburgers with me. Thanks for being a Donnie girl so I could have Joey all to myself. You've got the right stuff.

THE
BEST WORST
SUMMER

There were so many things I thought
would happen that summer.
Never did I imagine I'd lose my best friend.

CHAPTER ONE

This is the absolute worst summer in the history of summers.

Many years from now, song and poems will be written about it. History books will need to be updated to include this terrible, horrible, no good, very bad time. (Sorry, Alexander; one entire summer outdoes a measly day.)

In the olden days—like, last year—I would spend my time hanging out with my best friend, Lily. We'd have epic sleepovers. An entire week at an amazing soccer camp. Our regional championship soccer team would meet up for pizza every Saturday. My summers were THE BEST.

Now this one is THE WORST.

All because my mom decided to move us from our home in Minneapolis—a place where things actually happen—to Lake Springs, Minnesota, where absolutely nothing does. Seriously. The town has eight thousand people. That's it. And from our first drive through the mostly abandoned three blocks of downtown, none appeared to be my age.

They were probably all off with their own best friends.

I miss Lily.

"Be positive. This can be good," my mom said to me about a zillion times as I packed up my stuff.

Good for *her*, she meant. Mom got an offer to be the dean of the English department at Great Lakes College. So we moved four hours away from our real lives to this new place that doesn't feel like home.

I straighten out my brand-new comforter now. It was a bribe. Gone are my worn rainbow sheets and pillows. Now I have pink and yellow daisies. The trade-off: new bedding for ripping me away from my life. How exactly is that fair?

I take a picture of my new room and send it off to Lily, even though she won't get my messages for three more days. She's off at soccer camp, where it's technology-free. It's been the longest four days of my life. When she finally gets her phone back, she's going to have forty bajillion messages from me. That's *not* an exaggeration. I had sent mostly pictures: My old bedroom, empty except for a few boxes. The moving truck. A tear-streaked selfie the first night in this new house two days ago.

Lily promised to send me a postcard (it's basically her only option since it's like we're living in the Middle Ages or something). I've basically been stalking the mailman, desperate for any connection to my closest friend. To my former life. The one I actually liked.

And now . . .

Laughter booms from next door. "Dude, that was awesome!" my older brother, Jackson, calls out.

He's been basically hiding out in his room since we got here, headphones on, playing some game where he pretends to be like an elf or something with all his friends back home.

At least some things haven't changed for one of us.

With nothing else to do, I grab my soccer ball and head downstairs. Dad is sitting at the dining room table with *his* headphones on, working away at his computer. His advertising firm agreed to let him continue his graphic design job by working remotely.

"Think of how great it'll be," he had said to me. "Your old man will be around more!"

That's great in theory and everything, but since we moved, he's been glued to his computer screen. He's here, but not really.

So I guess nothing's really changed for him either.

I head out to our backyard, another one of Mom's Lake Springs selling points. "Look at all the space you'll have!" We went from a small apartment in the heart of downtown Minneapolis to a two-story, three-bedroom house with a yard, but what's the point of having space if I don't have anybody to play with? All this room for me to be alone and miserable. Hooray.

I kick the soccer ball around, but it doesn't go far in the overgrown grass. My mind wanders to what Lily is doing right now at soccer camp. Maybe they're practicing speed drills. My stomach growls as I think of the tater tot casserole they sometimes serve at lunch, which is delicious—I mean, you can't really go wrong with tater tots, especially when they're covered in cheese. I loved camp so much I didn't mind how bruised my legs would get or how sore I'd feel at the end of the day.

I kick the ball hard, and it slams into the wooden fence that borders our backyard.

"We'll have to get you a net," Dad calls out from the back door. He rubs the stubble on his graying beard. "I guess I need to add 'lawnmower' to the list."

I shrug in response. I've been dealing with everything by giving my family the silent treatment. No one asked me if I wanted to move. They just did it. "How can we say no to such a great opportunity?" I was told over and over again. It seems pretty easy to me. It's a two-letter word: N-O. There doesn't seem to be anything "great" about it.

"Peyton, it's going to be okay," Dad tries to reassure me for the eight millionth time. "I know this is hard."

"This place is the worst!" I throw my head back. "I'm so *bored*."

I'm already caught up with all my favorite YouTubers. I've set up a group text with my friends from back home who aren't at soccer camp, but I don't have much to share except that I'm miserable. I've watched practically every US women's soccer video online. Twice.

I have run out of things to do.

"Bored?" The corner of Dad's lips turn up. "Well, we can fix that."

He disappears into the house and returns with some tools in his hand.

Ugh. Of course Dad's answer for boredom is to give me more chores. I unpacked my room in a day, but the family's to-do list is endless.

Dad gives me a small shovel and a pair of gardening gloves. "We need to clear these weeds." He says *we*, but I know he means *me*.

And here I didn't think this summer could possibly get worse. There needs to be a new phrase to describe it: worstest? The bummerist of summers?

I sink my knees in the dirt that lines the fence. Dad has grand plans for the backyard. "We can plant our own garden!" Again, he says *we*, but I have a feeling that will be all *me*. The girl with nothing else to do.

Weed by weed, I let out my frustration. A few are so stubborn I have to dig around them. I'm nearly halfway through, sweat dripping down my face, as I grab a big weed and pull. Nothing. It won't budge.

I take the shovel and dig around it.

Pull.

Nothing.

I dig some more, over a foot down, when my shovel makes contact with something. I clear the dirt to see a bright orange . . . thing. My hands push the dirt away from the top.

It's a Nike shoebox wrapped in plastic.

I take a step back.

Something has been buried in our backyard.

CHAPTER TWO

1989

"This is going to be THE BEST SUMMER EVER!" I scream in delight.

"The best!" my very best friend in the whole wide world, Jess, agrees. Of course she does; we agree on everything. It *is* going to be THE BEST!

"We have the entire summer!" I shout as I twirl around.

"The whole summer!" Jess says as she claps her hands excitedly.

"What should we do tomorrow?" I ask.

"We could go to the park!"

"Or the mall!"

"Or the pool!"

"Or the arcade!"

"Oh! I've got it." Jess's big brown eyes go wide. "We can stop at Book World and then go through our magazines at Wilz's!"

"Yes!" That's exactly what our official first day of summer needs. We'll get the latest *Bop* and *Tiger Beat* and then drink milkshakes at the soda fountain.

Could there even be a better first day? I don't think so!

Jess and I grab each other's hands and jump up and down in her driveway. We know we're being extra loud and hyper, but we're both so happy we don't have to be in school anymore where we have to behave and can't be silly and laugh and be ourselves.

Although, the only person I can truly be myself around is Jess. She doesn't make fun of me when I laugh so hard I let out a huge snort. Or when I get super excited when specific songs come on the radio. Or about the fact that sometimes there are certain things I don't want to talk about.

Jess just knows this stuff. She's not only my best friend, but she's also *the* best friend any person could ever have.

"And I want a piano concert," Jess adds.

"Of course," I reply with a deep bow like the kind I'll do onstage one day, after performing some super-hard piano piece with an orchestra and everything.

Jess's dad comes out of their house. "Good afternoon, Mel."

"Hi, Dr. Miller," I reply.

"*Dude*," Jess says in an exaggerated Bill and Ted voice. "I'm the only one allowed to call Melissa *Mel*—you know that."

"Yeah, *duuuude*," I reply.

He holds up his hands in surrender. "My apologies, Melissa and Jessica. You two look lovely."

"Thank you!" We both twirl around.

Jess is wearing a black dress with a wide red belt and puffy rainbow sleeves, her sleek black hair pulled up high in a red scrunchie. I have on an acid-wash denim skirt with my brand-new pink-and-blue paisley vest. My brown permed hair is half pulled back in a pink hair clip.

We look absolutely tubular.

"Are you guys ready to go?" he asks.

"We were born ready," we reply at the same time before cracking up. "*One, two, three, owe me a Coke!*"

School has been out for only three hours, and already this summer is totally awesome.

"Come on, birthday girl." Jess's mom opens the door to their red Cutlass Supreme.

"You look so pretty, Mrs. Miller," I tell her. Mrs. Miller is like a model. Her strawberry blond hair is always feathered to perfection, and today she's wearing a pink-and-white-striped button-down shirt over a pink polo shirt—collars popped, of course—and a bolo tie just like the one Debbie Gibson wore in the last issue of *Big Bopper.*

"Hey, what about me?" Dr. Miller asks as he twirls around in his boring business suit. He pretends to flip his hair, even though he's bald. "Do *I* look pretty?"

"Gag me with a spoon, Dad!" Jess exclaims. "He's so embarrassing," she whispers as we pile into the back seat.

"Oh, he's wearing the *beeper*," I whisper back in awe to Jess. Dr. Miller is so important that if there's an emergency at the hospital, his pager beeps, and it shows the phone number he's supposed to call right away. It's only ever gone off once when I've been with them, and we had to stop by a pay phone. I think it's so cool. It's like he's a spy.

(Really, he's an ear, nose, and throat doctor.)

"Okay! Back to our plans." Jess is always great about focusing on the most important matters at hand. And right now it's how we're going to spend our summer vacation.

Jess's dad turns on the radio, and classical music floods the car. Jess puts her hands over her ears. "Dad, it's my birthday! Don't I get to decide what we listen to?"

"Oh, is that the rule?" He chuckles lightly as he turns onto the main road in downtown Lake Springs.

"Daaaad," Jess groans.

"I wonder what I should put on. Would you like to listen to some good old classic rock?"

Jess throws her head back. "Not even."

"You know what they say . . ." I give her a grin.

"Parents just don't understand!" Jess and I finish together.

"When does school start again?" Dr. Miller asks with a wink.

Mrs. Miller pushes Jess's cassette into the car's tape deck. "Stop teasing the girls."

Jess and I squeal with delight before we sing along to the "oh, oh, oh-oh-ohs" of "You Got It (The Right Stuff)" by our favorite band in the universe, New Kids on the Block.

Dr. Miller speeds up the car as we make our way to Jess's

birthday dinner, her first celebration of the summer. Today— June 16—is the day she was born, in Korea, eleven years ago. For her birthday, Jess gets to pick whatever she wants to do, so we're going to Leo's Italian Eatery, just the four of us. On August 28, she celebrates her adoption day with a big party of the extended Miller family.

So each summer starts and ends with celebrating my amazing best friend.

"Just try to use your inside voices," her dad says as we walk into the restaurant. It's not like Jess and I don't know how to behave, but it's the start of summer.

No more pencils. No more books. No more teacher's dirty looks.

I like school. And books. But you know what I like even better? An entire summer with nothing else to do but hang out with my best friend.

After we settle in at the table and order our Shirley Temples, Dr. Miller hands Jess a colorful wrapped box. "Happy birthday, honey."

She tears into the wrapping paper. "Whoa!" she exclaims at the silver Kodak Disc camera. "Mel, we can document our entire summer! Say cheese!" She holds up the rectangular camera and snaps away.

A camera! I feel like we're so grown up. It's even better than the boom box I got for Christmas last year.

"Thanks so much!" Jess gets up and hugs both of her parents.

"My turn!" I nearly explode as I take her gift out of my pocket. I hate keeping anything from Jess, and I've wanted to shout about it since my mom took me to the mall last weekend.

Jess bounces in her seat as she rips the Snoopy wrapping paper. She opens up the box and lets out a scream that makes her parents recoil, but me so happy. "It's perfect!"

She holds up the gift to show her parents. It's two gold necklaces that, together, form a heart which says, "BEST FRIENDS." She takes one of the necklaces and puts it around her neck and then hands the other to me so I can do the same.

"I'm so glad you like it."

"Like it? I LOVE it!" She gives me a hug.

"Well, I think we need to capture this," Dr. Miller says as he takes out his own camera. Unlike Jess's new one, Dr. Miller has a Polaroid, so we can have the photo right away.

Jess scoots her chair next to mine, and we wrap our arms around each other as he clicks the button. The picture comes out of the camera, and he hands it to me since he knows how much I like to watch it develop—it's like magic right before my eyes.

As I wait for the off-white square to show me and Jess smiling, Jess looks down at the necklace.

"Mel, I swear to you that I'm never taking this off. Ever."

CHAPTER THREE

I guess this is also the summer where I dig up a dead pet.

Cool.

I stare at the orange shoebox. It doesn't look like the kind I have in my closet. It has the Nike logo on the sides, but the top has a world map. Maybe it was some special edition. Which would also make an appropriate coffin for a small animal. Fun times.

There appear to be some markings and maybe stickers on the box. It's hard to see through the plastic bag.

Dread fills me as I realize there's only one way to know for sure. I cautiously pull the box out of the dirt. It's surprisingly light. A few things rattle around as I set it down on the grass.

There's a possibility the box is going to smell horrid when I remove the protective wrapping. I lean back . . . and back . . . as I unwrap the plastic. I scrunch up my nose, anticipating the smell of rotting flesh or something. *Why did I think this was a good idea?*

The box is out of the plastic, and it smells . . . fine. Well, as fine as something that's been buried in the ground for a while can.

One of my questions is answered. There *are* stickers— some flat, some puffy—stuck around the outside: a rainbow unicorn, a strawberry that says "berry good," a yellow smiley face with "DINO-MITE!," the Smurfs, and a few characters I recognize from the Pac-Man game my dad has on his phone. He's always telling Jackson that he used to play video games "back in the day." I tried it once, and it was so boring. All you do is move a Pac-Man around, avoid ghosts, and eat dots. Since it didn't involve pretending to be some gnome, Jackson gave up after two seconds. My dad said it was "a dark day" as a father. Whatever that means.

On the top of the box are two swirly marks made with black marker. I trace the lines. I'm pretty sure it's cursive, as it looks a lot like the signatures my parents use for school forms. My last school didn't teach cursive, which upset my mom. She said if my new school didn't, she was going to show me. I didn't really care since I never really needed it. Until now, I guess.

My stomach ties up in knots as I think about going to a new school. Being in a new house has been hard enough. I don't even want to think about going into sixth grade not knowing anybody.

I study the two words. I wonder if someone signed the box. One of the words starts with an "M"—that's easy enough—but the other is difficult. Both have the letters "E" and "I," but that's about all I can figure out.

Okay, this box has names and stickers. It doesn't smell. Do I open it up?

How could I not?

I mean, what else do I have going on today, or tomorrow, or this entire summer?

I reach my hand out to lift the cover.

"What's that?" Jackson calls out from the door. My hand jerks away as I stifle a yelp.

"Ah, I found it in the garden," I reply with a dismissive shrug. It's the first time Jackson has started a conversation with me since we moved. He and I don't really do big talks, or any talks really. Most of his friends are virtual— knights, wizards, soldiers—while I prefer my company in person.

I shudder as I remind myself that things with Lily are now only going to be virtual too: texts, chats, et cetera. Mom promised I could go visit her before school starts, but it doesn't change the fact that we now live four hours apart.

Might as well be four billion hours.

Jackson takes a few steps closer while studying the box through his long brown bangs. "Oh, it's probably some dead pet."

Probably. *Didn't curiosity kill the cat? What if it* is *a dead cat?*

"Yeah, I'm going to throw it out," I lie.

I *am* going to open it, but it's something I want to do by myself. I want to know what's inside, and there's this part of me that needs to keep whatever it is from Jackson. Besides, he has his gaming friends while I feel like I have nothing.

"Yeah, don't get like rabies or whatever." He laughs because everything is a joke to him. "Later," he says with a nod as the screen door rattles behind him.

Jackson does have a point, so I'm glad I'm wearing the gardening gloves, *just* in case something is in there. I gently lift up the corner of the lid . . . and then immediately pull my hand away.

Okay, I need to treat this like ripping off a bandage. Just do it quickly and get it over with.

I take my hand and flip up the lid to find . . . not a dead animal, but junk.

On top is a piece of paper with letters on it:

FJ KLQ DLFKD QL JV DOXKAJLQEBOP. TBOB
IBXSFKD JV AXA. FQP DLQQBK YXA. FJ KLQ
XIILTBA QL ZXII VLR, YRQ FSB IBCQ JV
KBZHIXZB CLO TEBK TB PBB BXZE LQEBO
XDXFK. FII YB XQ JV JLJP YBPQ COFBKAP
ELRPB, ZBZFIFX MXIRZEKFXH FK TXRTXQLPX, TF.
ZLJB CFKA JB. VLRO YCC, XITXVP.

So that makes zero sense, and it's not even remotely helpful. It's probably some foreign language. Or, oh! Maybe it's a secret code.

I start going through all of the items and placing them on the grass beside me.

A small, light brown teddy bear with a white bow wrapped around its neck.

A picture of two girls around my age—one white with curly brown hair, the other Asian with black hair in a high ponytail—and a date written below: June 16, 1989.

Wow, 1989! I wonder if all this stuff is that ancient. It might be worth something!

A picture collage of a bunch of boys who look hilarious: one has a skinny braid coming from the back of his head, another is wearing a hat with the top cut off revealing his curly hair, and another is wearing overalls without a shirt on. So basically, boys have always been super weird.

A purple, pink, and white friendship bracelet. Now *this* makes me excited, since it's just like the ones we made at camp a few years ago. Maybe I'll make a new one for Lily. I'm not super crafty, but I can do a braid. Not like it'll top the matching bracelets Lily and I currently wear: narrow leather purple straps with silver engraved plates that say, "L+P."

A ticket stub for the movie *Batman*. My visions of a jackpot fade . . . I guess not everything is from 1989, since

Jackson was just talking about some Batman movie on the long drive here.

A scribbled receipt for two cheeseburgers, two fries, and two Cherry Cokes at some place called the Kitchen Corner. The total was six dollars, so I'm back to thinking this has to be from a long, *long* time ago.

A receipt from a place called Book World.

A coaster from Wilz's Drug Store. What kind of drug store would have a restaurant in it? Ew.

There are a few plastic things—one is a clear plastic rectangle with pink, yellow, and blue designs about the size of a deck of cards with brown ribbons wrapped around two yellow wheels inside, and the other is this flat black weird square shape thing with a yellow sticker that says, "Kodacolor disc"—I have no idea what they are.

And finally, a necklace. It has a broken heart that says, "ST ENDS."

Wait a second. I know this one! It's half of a best friend necklace.

What I don't know is why anybody would bury this random stuff.

Something on the inside lid of the box catches my eye. It's handwriting. My stomach plunges as I read it:

I'm so sorry. Please forgive me.

I look between the necklace and the picture of the two

friends. I squint at the photo and see both are wearing their halves.

Now one is buried in a box with an apology.

I go through all the items again. My mind buzzes trying to make sense out of what this means. I feel like I have to understand so I don't make the same mistakes with Lily.

It comes to me like a lightning bolt.

I now have a plan for the summer: I'm going to figure out what happened back in 1989.

CHAPTER FOUR

1989

I cannot even hold my excitement as I come down for breakfast on what is going to be the first full day of the best summer.

"Morning, sweetheart." Mom greets me with a smile, a glass of orange juice, and a strawberry Pop-Tart. "Sorry I couldn't make breakfast. Your dad had to go into work early, and I have an appointment I need to leave for soon."

"It's okay." It's more than okay since this means frosting for breakfast.

Mom shakes her head as she laughs. "Oh, I'm sure it is. So what plans do you and Jessica have for today?"

"We're going to Book World and then out to lunch. And just biking around."

"Try to not spend your allowance all at once. Those magazines get expensive."

"*Mooooom.*" Yeah, I probably spend most of my money on

magazines, but it's New Kids on the Block! I need to see all their latest pictures and interviews. Waiting four weeks for new magazines has been torture!

"*Meliiiiisaaaa*," Mom echoes. "I'm sure you're going to have a great day. You and Jessica remind me so much of Ceci and me when we were your age."

I nod along because Mom says that all the time. Her best friend, Cecilia, lives near Milwaukee, and Mom only sees her a couple of times a year. I don't understand how you can be so far away from your best friend.

Jess and I have it all planned out. We're going to go to the same college, where we'll be roommates, and then move into a two-bedroom apartment in some big city. Maybe Minneapolis so we'll still be close to our families. We'll travel the world together. Our first trip will be to Korea so Jess can see where she was born. We'll be maid of honor at each other's weddings and then live next door so our kids can grow up together, too. It's going to be totally awesome!

Mom brushes her finger against my cheek. "You have fun today. Be sure to be back in time for dinner."

I shove the rest of the Pop-Tart into my mouth as I run into the garage and grab my bike. I ride the four blocks to the halfway point between my house and Jess's. She's already waiting for me. Jess is always early, while I tend to get a little distracted.

"I had a Pop-Tart for breakfast," I say as explanation for not being on time.

"Jealous! Mom made me eat a banana with my Cheerios."

"Honey Nut?"

She grimaces. "Regular."

Jess's parents are strict and won't let her have sugar cereal—and for them that means any cereal where sugar is one of the first two ingredients. Meanwhile, my dad will enjoy a bowl of Frosted Flakes himself. Whenever Jess stays over, she gets to have the good stuff in the morning. Her favorite cereal is Lucky Charms because every meal should include marshmallows, *especially* breakfast.

"You know what this means?"

"Sleepover!" we both say at the same time. Again! "*One, two, three, owe me a Coke!*"

Since we pretty much share a brain, Jess and I owe each other like a zillion Cokes.

"Yes! Tonight?" she asks.

I pause. It's something I rarely do around Jess. She bites her bottom lip as she waits for me to respond.

"Um, let me check to see what night works best," I finally reply. If it were up to me, I would have Jess over every night. It's just that my dad can get kind of cranky when he's working a lot, and it's best to have a sleepover when he's out with his bowling team or something. He doesn't like a lot of noise. I have to practice my piano when he's at work and wear headphones if I want to listen to music in my room.

I don't have to explain any of this to Jess, though, because she just knows.

"That's okay. You can spend the night at my house whenever you want," she offers.

"We should do it every night!"

"That would be so major!" Jess laughs before she turns serious. "Although I don't think we'd get much sleep."

This is true. Whenever we stay the night at the other's house, we stay up almost all night—sometimes until *midnight*—talking and laughing and just being ourselves.

"I'll ask my mom, but I'm sure it's fine," I say. I'm already excited. Jess has a huge bed with fluffy pillows.

"Yes!" Jess takes her small pink backpack off and pulls out her camera. "But first, I have to take a picture to commemorate the first day of our best summer ever. Smile!"

She points her camera at me, and I stick my tongue out. "Perfect!" She laughs. "I can't wait to get this developed."

"I call doubles!"

"Of course you'll get the extra set. I really want to take a picture every day, but film is expensive. So we'll do it once a week."

"Oh, then we can do a photo album." This most excellent summer needs to be fully documented. "We'll have to get someone to take our photo so we can both be in it."

Jess groans. "I should've waited until lunch."

"Next week!" We have all summer to fill her camera with pictures and memories.

I get excited when my parents bring home photos after getting them developed. There's always a surprise. Sometimes good—a shot we forgot about. Sometimes bad—someone's eyes will be closed. I wish there was a faster way to tell if a picture turned out okay.

"Besides," Jess says as she pushes off on her bike. We begin to pedal toward downtown. "I need to save all my money for magazines and cheeseburgers and milkshakes."

"Yes!" I agree. Photos are great and all, but our summer plans require cold, hard cash.

"What magazine are you going to get?" Jess asks.

"*Duh*. Whichever has the most pictures of Joey!" Joey McIntyre is my favorite member of New Kids on the Block. He's the youngest and has the sweetest voice and these bright blue eyes. *Swoon!* Every month Jess and I stop by Book World to get the newest magazines: *Bop, Big Bopper, Teen Beat, Tiger Beat*. We trade pictures to put up on our bedroom walls. Even though our rooms are very different—I have a twin bed pushed into the corner of a tiny space, while she has a princess canopy bed and a large white dresser and desk—the walls look the same. Every corner (and now my ceiling) is covered with pictures of our future husbands.

"*No duh*," Jess replies with a laugh. "I can't believe I even asked. I have a bunch of birthday money, so I'm going to get them all. And you can have the Joey pictures."

"And you can have my Jordan ones." Jess's favorite New

Kid is Jordan Knight, just reason number one million and one why we get along so well; we don't have to fight over boys. (Not that we fight about *anything*.)

We turn the corner on Elm Street and stop as we see construction vehicles in our school's parking lot.

"Whoa," Jess says as we bike to the fence. We watch as a jackhammer starts tearing through the concrete.

"I wonder when they're going to bury our time capsule," I say. When our school got the funds to build a new playground, they decided that they'd bury a time capsule before they poured the new asphalt. Each grade put an item in. Fifth grade was assigned something featuring a prominent current event, so we added the front page of the *Daily Register* from when the Exxon Valdez oil spill happened a couple of months ago off the coast of Alaska. It was so sad seeing all the ducks and animals covered in oil. Our science teacher, Mrs. Vesley, said it was the perfect choice as the world probably won't be so dependent on oil in a few decades.

"Can you imagine what Lake Springs will be like when the box is dug up?" Jess asks. "We'll be old. Like thirty or something."

"Our husbands will be bald," I reply with a fake shiver.

"Jordan is never going to lose that amazing hair." Jess bats her eyelashes.

"True."

"No matter when they find it, we'll still be best friends."

"Also true." We stand in silence as we watch our playground get ripped up.

"Oh! What if the construction guys find an old time capsule now?" I ask, because that would be so righteous. "Maybe someone had the same idea when they paved this playground the first time. Wouldn't that be cool?"

"It would." Then Jess's eyes go wide. "Oh! Oh! I have the best idea, Mel."

Knowing Jess it's going to be amazing.

"Okay, what if *we* did a time capsule of our summer and buried it for someone to find? We can put all our favorite stuff in there and leave a note. What do you think?"

I can barely contain my excitement. "Um, I think it's the best idea EVER!"

CHAPTER FIVE

Fun fact: basically, the internet wasn't around in 1989.

Pretty much nothing was back then. No Google. No YouTube. Not even Facebook, which is something my parents use, so I figured it's been around since the beginning of time.

My whole plan for finding out who these two girls were has turned up a big, fat nothing. Not like there was much of a plan. I thought if I searched "Lake Springs" and "1989" online, I could maybe find, ah, some clue. Like a picture of the girls with their names so I could, I don't know, go on Facebook and . . .

Yeah, so, basically, I have no idea what to do.

But, seriously, what did people even do back before the internet? And I thought *my* summer was boring.

I study the photos of the two girls. Maybe they still live in town and I can find them.

My focus shifts to the Asian girl. My old school had some diversity—Lily is Latinx, and three of the girls on our soccer team are also people of color, including Amal, who wears her hijab while we play—but from the little I've seen of Lake Springs, it's a pretty white town.

If my suspicions about the population holds, this girl—now a woman—would stand out. I guess I'll keep my eye out for an Asian American female in her forties. And then what? Go up to her and ask if she's this girl? Yeah, like that's not racist.

Maybe it's best for me to focus on the items instead of the people.

"Dad?" I call out from my bedroom before walking downstairs to the living room/Dad's office. His headphones are on as he stares at a logo design on his big computer screen. He doesn't hear me.

I tap his shoulder, and he jumps a bit. "Oh, sorry, P. What's up? Did you finish the backyard?"

"Yes—"

"Okay, I'm almost done with this. Just give me a couple of . . ." His attention drifts off as an email notification pings.

I know how this goes. He says it'll be a couple of minutes, and he'll get caught up in something else. I'd never bother him when he was at his old office, but since he started work-ing from home, it seems all he does is work. He's on his com-puter all day, even going back after dinner. He and Jackson both glued to their screens. (At least Dad's getting paid, I guess.)

But I have my own work to do and need his help.

"What's this?" I hold out the small plastic rectangle with the two little wheels. I think I've seen it before on some TV show or something, and it might play movies? Like I remember my parents talking about VCRs at one point. But it also says "Scotch" on it, so maybe it's just boring old tape.

Dad does a double take. "Oh, wow. Where on earth did you get this?"

"In the backyard," I reply, because it's the truth. I just don't tell him about the box. It's the same as with Jackson—I want to have something for myself.

Dad takes the thing in his hand, and the skin around his eyes crinkles as he smiles broadly. He even ignores another ping from his computer. "This is a tape."

"So, it's a tape dispenser?"

He laughs lightly. "No, it's a cassette tape."

I give him a blank stare because I have no clue what that means.

"It plays music . . . ," he continues.

I look at the plastic container. It doesn't have any speakers or a place to plug in headphones. "Where does the music come from?"

Dad shakes his head as he takes off his glasses. He rubs

his eyes. "It's something you put in a tape deck in a stereo or a boom box."

So, yeah, that still answers absolutely nothing. "And a boom box is . . . ?"

"Oh, Peyton, stop making your dad feel old!" He opens up the case and takes out the cassette. "Who are M and J?"

He hands me the cassette tape back, and I see there's neat printing that says, "M + J's best summer ever mix" on one side.

I shrug. I have the exact same question.

But I also have another one. "What's a mix?"

"Oh, you kids today have missed out. It's a playlist. You would take this cassette and record songs on it. I'll have you know that I once wooed your mother with a mix CD on one of our first dates." He gives me a wink.

Gross.

"So do you have a tape deck or boom box?" We have one of those digital speakers in the living room that plays whatever you tell it to, because we do not live in the Dark Ages. But I assume that won't work. "I want to hear what's on it."

"No. My first car had a tape deck, but ours only have Bluetooth now." Honestly, it's as if he's speaking in a foreign language. He grimaces at my expression. "Stop looking at me like I'm some old dude. Your grandparents had an eight-track in their van!"

So now I'm even more confused. Eight-track? Boom box? I thought I'd be able to easily figure out *one* item in the box, but I guess not.

"What's the matter, P?" Dad takes in my defeated expression.

Oh, nothing. Just that I'm giving up hope on the box. It's like my default setting for the summer.

"Nothing's wrong," I lie. "I'm just curious what's on it."

Dad leans back in his office chair. "Well, someone has to have a tape deck in this town."

Problem is, we don't know anybody here.

He holds up his finger. "Don't you worry, we'll figure this out. I'll text your mother. There has to be a tape deck at the college. At least in the library."

"The library!" I perk up. "I can go to the library here and see if they have one." Mom's campus is nearly a twenty-minute drive, and who knows when I'll be able to go there. I want to listen to the cassette tape now. It's not like I have anything else to do. There are only so many drills I can run in the back-yard and videos to watch. It's always better to do those things with Lily anyways.

Dad turns to type into his computer. "Well, let's give them a call first." He pulls up the Lake Springs Public Library website and then picks up his phone. "Hello, we're new to town, and I'm just wondering if your library has a cassette player. My daughter— Oh, that's wonderful!"

Yes! The library to the rescue! It's the first time I feel appreciation for anything in this town.

Dad continues, "Great! We'll swing by to get our library cards, and my daughter can listen to this *ancient device* she found." He then laughs at something on the other line. "I know. Nothing like a child to make you feel old."

I roll my eyes as he hangs up.

"Can we go now?" I ask, bouncing on the balls of my feet. It feels nice to have something to do.

"Can't. I've got a video call in a few minutes." Dad gives me a small smile.

"Well, how far is it?" This town isn't that big. I can probably walk or bike there.

"I'm not letting you go to the library by yourself."

"Dad, I'm *eleven*."

"Yes, and I'm not letting my daughter wander around alone in a new town."

All during the move, Mom and Dad kept saying I'm a "young lady" now and that I shouldn't throw fits and could pack up my room. But I'm apparently not big enough to go out on my own.

"Can we go tomorrow?"

Dad pulls up his calendar on his screen. "Sure."

"In the morning."

"Okay."

"*Promise.*" I know he says now that he can do it tomorrow, but something always seems to come up with work.

"I promise."

"Pinky promise." I hold out my pinky.

"Oh well, this is serious." Dad clears his throat, stands up, and gets down on bended knee. "Peyton Cassandra Howard, on this day, the nineteenth of June, I do solemnly swear to take you to the library tomorrow morning."

This time my eye roll is more exaggerated, but I feel a glimmer of hope.

Tomorrow, I may get some answers.

CHAPTER SIX

1989

"Where are we going to bury *you know*?"

A few heads at Prairie View Park turn our way as Jess covers her mouth and starts to laugh.

"I can't believe you just shouted that!" I pretend to scold her. "Everybody probably thinks we're up to no good."

It wouldn't be the first time. People are always giving us weird looks when we're simply being us. The only people who truly get Jess and me are Jess and me.

"*Or* they'll stay away so we can have the swings all to ourselves."

"Oh, good idea!" I kick my feet out so I can fly even higher.

It's a beautiful Tuesday afternoon, so we rode our bikes to our favorite park. It has this huge new jungle gym with slides and places to climb. Jess and I are a bit too old for that, but we do love to swing side by side.

"We could bury it in our backyard," Jess offers. "Even though I keep begging Dad to build a pool."

"We'll wear him down eventually." Every time Jess's mom gets ready to drive us to the town pool, we make sure to talk about how we'd spend more time at the Millers' if they had their own. "We can bury it at my house."

Our backyard is a lot smaller than the Millers'. So there's a better chance of someone eventually discovering it.

Then the perfect place hits me. "Oh! We can bury it in the garden against the fence. There's that shady area in the corner where the Wilkins' tree covers it."

"Sounds perfect." Jess jumps off the swing and lands softly. She runs over to a woman who is sitting on a bench next to an empty stroller. "Excuse me, ma'am, could you please take our picture?"

Jess also has the best manners.

The woman gets ready to take the picture as Jess jumps back on the swing, her feet on the saddle. I also stand up in the seat. We both smile widely.

After the photo is taken, I come up with another idea. "Why don't we leave a set of the photos we take this summer in our time capsule?" We've already decided to include magazines, a mix tape, and maybe some drawings.

"Oh, great idea."

"Why thank you!" I jump down from the swing. I throw

my arms up when I land like I'm Phoebe Mills jumping off the balance beam at the Olympics last year.

"Perfect landing," Jess admires.

I do a deep bow, imagining an Olympic medal dangling from my neck although I can't even do a cartwheel.

"Hey, guys!"

We look over to see our friend Amy Campbell coming over from the activity area.

Jess waves excitedly at Amy as she skips toward us, her long, curly blond hair bouncing behind her. I've always been so jealous of Amy's hair. I have to get my hair permed, but hers is natural.

"Are you guys here for crafts?" Amy asks us. "Kristi was supposed to come, but she isn't feeling well."

"We're not doing parks and rec this summer," I state with a voice that I'm hoping shows how mature Jess and I are for doing something different this year. We're practically teenagers! In like two years, anyway. Although, I am a little jealous as I look over and see they're doing plaster of Paris molds with seashells. Arts and crafts were always my favorite activities. I still have the dream catcher I made last summer.

"Oh." Amy's face falls. "Well, I was going to call you guys later to invite you to a sleepover on Saturday."

"That sounds like so much fun," Jess says before I have a chance to react. "I can't wait!"

"Yes! I'm so excited you can make it," Amy exclaims. She then turns to me. "Can you come, Melissa?"

"Of course she can!" Jess replies. "Right, Mel?"

"Oh, um . . ."

I like Amy. I like sleepovers. It's just . . . around Jess, I can be me. I can tell her anything, and she won't judge me. I can be silly and goofy and loud. I don't feel like that around other people. Playing during recess is one thing; a sleepover is entirely different. Maybe it's because I'm an only child, but I'll admit, I don't like to share Jess.

"Mel?" Jess bites her lip as she looks at me expectantly.

I know I'm being silly. It's one sleepover. It's not like Amy could ever take my place.

"Yeah, sure, great."

Jess and Amy start talking excitedly about what movie to rent, and I can't help but feel a pang of jealousy watching them go back and forth.

A group of boys who are a year younger than us walk past. "Oh, look who it is!" One of them—this boy named Doug who lives around the block from me—squints his eyes at Jess and pulls them to the sides with his fingers. "*Herroooo*," he says in an awful accent.

The smile on Jess's face disappears.

"Herroooo. When are you going back to China?" another says, and they start laughing.

A lump forms in my throat as I feel so helpless to

stop them. Jess has shrunk into herself, and I need to—I have to—

Amy steps between Jess and the boys while I remain frozen. "Just shut up, you jerks! Go away. You're being mean!"

"Hey, you got something on your forehead," Doug says as he points at Amy.

The other one takes an exaggerated inhale, then plugs his nose. "Did you stick your head in a toilet?"

Amy shifts her bangs to cover her forehead—where she has a large dark birthmark in the corner—but doesn't move. "If you don't leave right this instant, I'm going to go over and tell Miss Parker you're being awful."

The boys look over to the crafts area and shrug before leaving, but not without a few more insults tossed our way.

"Ugh, they're so mean," Amy says as she hugs Jess. "Are you okay?"

Jess nods. "I guess."

"Don't listen to anything those boys say. They're always following me home from school saying things about my birthmark. It's like way to be boys, *boys*."

The tiniest smile spreads on Jess's face. "Thank you for standing up for me."

And I just stand there feeling guilty I didn't say anything. I know it upsets Jess when people do that. I should've told those boys to shut up and that they're a bunch of bullies, or better yet, I should've gone over to Miss Parker and gotten help myself.

But I didn't.

I did nothing.

Maybe I'm not such a best friend, after all.

I felt a little off after our encounter with those boys and Amy. I couldn't help but feel that I wasn't a good friend. That I should have stuck up for Jess. That I really don't want to go to this sleepover.

But playing the piano always makes me feel better.

"Encore! Encore!" Jess applauds. "Can you play the one with the da-da-da-das that I like?"

I nod as I pull out the Beethoven book from the storage cupboard in my piano bench.

After the park, we came over to my house so I could give Jess a piano recital. We usually end with us singing along to some of the Debbie Gibson and New Kids sheet music she gave me for my birthday in April.

"You're *so* good," Jess says as she pulls her chair in even closer. She likes to study my fingers as they move across the keys.

"Thanks," I reply and force a smile. I flip to "Für Elise" and begin playing it.

I'm a pretty average student. I'm not like Jess, who takes advanced science classes. I'm okay in gym. But music is what makes me special. When I sit down at the piano, I only have to concentrate on the notes in front of me. Everything else fades away.

I push my worries aside as I play one of my favorite pieces. Jess even lets out a little "whoa" when my fingers fly up the keyboard during a quick run.

I find myself sitting a little taller. Anytime I feel blue, I play the piano. I only wish I didn't have to cut back on my lessons because we don't have money for—as my dad calls it—"silly things." Like piano music. Like me.

When I finish the last chord, Jess jumps up and starts singing the melody as she dances around. "It's so pretty! Maybe I should take up ballet so I can dance while you play?"

I nod as I flip through my book to see what I should play next.

"Hey." Jess sits down on the bench next to me. "Are you okay?"

I keep my focus on my fingers on the keys.

"I'm . . . ," I begin, but I could never lie to Jess. Not that I ever want to hide anything from her. "I'm really sorry."

Jess bites her lip. "Why are you sorry?"

Where to begin?

"I should've said something to those guys. It wasn't okay what they did." My chest feels heavy knowing that I wasn't there for my best friend when she needed me.

Jess frowns. "I'm just so tired of everybody assuming all Asian people are the same. I'm Korean, not Chinese."

I know how much it upsets her to be wrongly identified.

More than once a waiter has assumed I was Dr. and Mrs. Miller's daughter since we're all white. Nobody ever thinks I'm not a member of my family.

I also know about my birth family. My father's father came from County Cork in Ireland and immigrated to America when he was three. My mom's family is from all over Europe: England, Germany, and Yugoslavia. They even did a chart once so I would know that I'm two-fifth Irish, and one-fifth this or that. (Math is more Jess's thing.)

All Jess knows is that she was adopted from the South Korean city of Busan. That's it. She doesn't know anything about her birth parents. She's never been to Korea or met anybody who has. She confided in me that she keeps the "K" volume of the *Encyclopedia Britannica* under her bed so she can look at pictures of Korea and scan the faces of the people.

There's so much that I love about Jess that has nothing to do with where she came from. The way she doesn't get self-conscious when we're out somewhere and she laughs or dances. How she's fearless in gym class—she'll go rushing after the ball, while I'm worried I'll get hurt or fall on my butt. How she's not only the youngest member, but the only girl in Science Explorers, a club that competes in science fairs. How she's so generous with all that she has, but doesn't make me feel like I have less than her. Still, I hope one day she gets the chance to find out more about where she's from.

"You're amazing," I tell her for like the four billionth time, because *duh*. "And anybody who doesn't know that is an idiot."

"I mean, *no duh*, they're boys, so total idiots."

"Exactly!"

She puts her chin on my shoulder. "I wish I didn't feel so alone sometimes."

I open my mouth, but close it. I don't know what to say. I didn't know Jess felt lonely. She's not alone. She has me. But maybe she means lonely because she's the only Korean person in town.

"Do you—" I start to ask, but she cuts me off.

"Oh, play this one!" she says as she points to a sonata.

I thought I knew Jess better than anybody. She can tell if I'm upset by a single look.

But I guess I don't know my best friend as well as I thought.

CHAPTER SEVEN

I'm finally excited to be in this new town.

Dad and I pull up to the library, which is only a dozen blocks away from our house. It's an older redbrick building that's a lot smaller than the library in my old neighborhood.

"Now, I have a call, but I will be back in an hour. Text me if you need anything. Do not—and I repeat—*do not* leave the library. Don't talk to strangers. Well, except the librarians. Be careful and—"

"*Daaaaaad*," I say, embarrassed that he's making a fuss. I've been to a library before.

Though, I was usually meeting Lily. Now it's only me.

We enter the building. Every inch is crammed with bookshelves—it's a glorious sight. Off to the right is the kids' room, and behind the front desk are rows and rows of books.

"Hello," Dad greets the librarian. "I called yesterday about the tape deck."

She gives us a warm smile as she helps us fill out forms to get library cards. She then leads me to a table filled with different equipment that looks like it belongs in some museum.

"Oh, wow, microfiche." Dad points at a giant screen with a wide back that looks to be about a gazillion years old.

"Yes, this hardly gets any use, but I can't bear to part with it," the librarian says with a frown.

"Ah, here it is!" Dad gestures for me to sit down in front of a big gray rectangle box. "Thanks so much for your help. I'm just going to be a few minutes away, but I told my daughter that she could ask you for help if she needs it."

"Absolutely, and it's so nice to meet you, Peyton." She gives me a nod before heading back to the front desk.

"So here's the deal, P." He presses a button on the machine, and a plastic drawer opens up. He takes the cassette tape and puts it in the drawer before closing it. "Okay, here you got your buttons. Play, stop—"

"Dad, I know what the buttons mean." *Please.* I have my own iPhone.

"Yes, but rewind and fast-forward work a little differently." He hits the button with two arrows pointing right, and the wheels on the tape go speeding by. "See, back in the day you had to scan for the next song. You couldn't just skip with a tap of a button."

That seems a bit tedious. At this point, I'm surprised there was even indoor plumbing thirty years ago.

Dad hits the stop button and puts the headphones on. "I want to make sure it's okay for you to listen to." A smile spreads on his face. "Ah, this brings back memories." He hits a few more buttons and bobs his head up and down. "You're going to get an education today about back when music was fun and you could understand the lyrics instead of all the fast-talking rap and K-pop you like."

"*Daaaaaaad.*" I pout as I hold out my hand. We came here so *I* could listen to the music. "Don't you have some important work call to get back to?"

That does it. He removes the headphones and hits the rewind button.

My heart speeds up as I watch the wheels go round and round. There's a high-pitched noise. What if this ancient machine breaks and I never find out what's on it? I jump when the tape suddenly stops and the button clicks off.

"Okay, kiddo." Dad puts the headphones on me. "Have a listen. I'll be back in an hour. Be smart and—"

"Got it," I reply as I hit play, waiting to see what's in store. He kisses me on the forehead before he walks away.

Static fills the earphones as I wait to see what M and J put on the tape.

Music starts, followed by a booming male voice. "*It's over-cast and raining, but we've got the latest from Paula Abdul to brighten up your day. You're listening to Z104.*"

A woman's voice starts singing, and I try to nod along,

but I'm confused why they wouldn't download a clean version of the song. Why would they want someone talking over it?

I take out the notebook I brought to start making a list of the songs. I have to pull out my phone and put the mic near the headphones so an app can tell me what's playing. The first is "Cold Hearted" by Paula Abdul. There's a weird pause, and another song comes on, but it seems like the beginning was cut off. At least there isn't somebody talking over it. It's a slower song, and a girl is singing in a high voice. I find out it's "I'll be Loving You (Forever)" by New Kids on the Block.

I continue my list of songs and artists: Richard Marx, Martika, Chicago . . . The only person I've heard of is Madonna. I'm going to download this playlist when I'm done.

My phone pings, and it's my dad checking in to make sure I'm still alive.

I moan as I reply that I'm fine and haven't even left the seat.

Then I hear a voice from someone closer to my age. "What are you doing?"

I look up and notice a boy sitting across from me. He's pale with sandy brown hair, a round face, and wire-rimmed glasses.

"Oh, I'm listening to music on a cassette tape."

His light green eyes go wide. "Wow, how retro of you."

"How do you know about cassette tapes?" I ask.

He looks shocked. "How do you *not* know?"

Maybe because I'm not fifty years old?

He laughs at my confused expression. "I get it. My grandpa's garage is like a museum. He loves repairing old things like record players and radios from back in the day. And then my mom will go on and on about the good old days and how things were simpler when she was my age."

"My dad looked so hurt when I had no idea what a cassette tape was," I admit.

"Ah, yes, I'm more than familiar with the how-dare-you-remind-me-that-I-am-no-longer-young look. The absolute betrayal." He leans back in his chair. "Are you new here? Not like I know everybody in Lake Springs, but I'm usually familiar with the library crowd."

"Yeah, my family and I just moved here from Minneapolis."

"Well, welcome to Lake Springs. It's not Minneapolis, but it's not as boring as it seems."

I lift my eyebrows at him. "I'll take your word for it because it seems pretty boring to me."

He nods as he pushes up the glasses on his nose. "Yeah, I found that you have to find the fun here. But we have some cool parks, and the library is good. We also have the best—and I do mean the absolute best—ice cream in the world. Not that I've traveled the world extensively, but I've been to *eight* states, and nothing has come close to Frannie's ice cream."

"Really?" I ask, because I love ice cream—I mean, who

doesn't? But I've had some pretty good ice cream, and I doubt a place in a tiny town could rival anything I've had in Minneapolis or any of the *nine* states I've been to.

"They have really great flavors that rotate. My favorite is a tie between peanut butter and pretzels and the breakfast bowl, which is basically sugar cereal in ice cream form. My mom is so uptight about sugar for breakfast, but lets me eat that. I'm not about to argue, you know?"

"DON'T I!" I say loudly before quickly covering my mouth.

It's this inside joke Lily and I have. Every time someone says "you know"—which people say *a lot*—we always reply loudly with "DON'T I!" And then she and I will crack up, while the other person looks as confused as this boy across from me. But he's not going to understand that, and now I'm just embarrassed, even though I do get what he's saying. So much for making a good impression with the first person in this town to talk to me.

I clear my throat. "Ah, yeah, so, um, that ice cream does sound good, but I'm allergic to peanuts."

He gives me a slow nod. "Ah, yes, the forbidden nut. If it makes you feel any better, my sister can't have gluten."

Oddly, it does. One of my (former) teammates was allergic to wheat. It made going out for pizza a little complicated.

"My last school had several kids with peanut allergies, so the entire school had to be nut-free," I say. A few of our classmates complained, but it made me feel safer knowing I wouldn't be exposed, even though my allergy is mild compared to some. I didn't even think about whether my new school is nut-free. I'm sure Mom and Dad have looked into it. I always carry an EpiPen in my backpack just in case.

I've heard stories of some schools having a table only for kids with peanut allergies. There are worse ways to make friends, I guess.

"Pretzels in ice cream sounds delicious, though." I think about how Lily and I can devour an entire bag of chocolate-covered pretzels after a game. "My favorite ice creams are with sweet-and-salty combinations."

"Yes, salted caramel—"

"The best!"

He nods appreciatively. "You've got some good taste. I'm Lucas, by the way."

"Hey, I'm Peyton. Do you go to St. Mary's?" I ask while nearly crossing my fingers, hoping I'll know at least one person before I start. There are three grade schools in the area, and then we all filter into one high school.

Lucas shakes his head. "I'm at St. John's."

Figures.

"But I have a buddy who goes to St. Mary's," Lucas adds, probably sensing that I'm bummed. "Connor's going into sixth grade. You?"

"Same!"

My phone pings again; it's Dad telling me he'll be here in fifteen and that he's coming in to get me and I should stay put. I groan. "My dad's being so annoyingly overprotective. Like I can't handle listening to music on my own or something."

"I can totally relate." Lucas gestures his chin to the corner.

I turn around to see a woman with the same light hair in a neat ponytail, reading a book. She looks up, and when she notices me, she jumps from her seat and practically sprints over.

"Well hello! I haven't seen you here before. I'm Lucas's mom, Holly." She reaches out her hand to shake.

"Hi, I'm Peyton. My family just moved here."

Okay, so I'm totally breaking Dad's rule about talking to strangers, but what am I supposed to do? Ignore Lucas and his mom? With my mom busy at the college, Dad glued to his computer, and Jackson not leaving his bedroom, *someone* in my family has to be social.

"Oh, how lovely!" She looks excitedly between Lucas and me. "I'm so happy to see Lucas making friends."

"*Mooooooom*," Lucas protests.

"Now, Lucas, it's important to be welcoming to a new family in town." She looks around the library. "Where are your parents? I'd love to meet them!" Everything is so bright and cheery with her. Lucas appears to find it annoying, but at least she's involved in his life.

"My dad's picking me up soon," I explain.

"Well, I'd love to meet him and maybe have your family over for dinner. Wouldn't that be fun, honey?"

"*Mooooooom*," Lucas whines again. "Do you think it would be possible to not embarrass me for one day? Just a single twenty-four-hour period. I think that's a reasonable request."

She shakes her head with a familiar expression, the same one that my dad had yesterday: *Kids, what are you going to do?*

It's something I think of often when dealing with my parents, because what can *I* do about *them*?

The phone in her hand rings. "Oh! I have to take this. One minute." She holds out her index finger as she walks away.

Lucas puts his head in his hands. "Feel free to escape now while she's occupied. I don't have that luxury."

Weirdly enough, I don't feel like leaving. I still have a few songs left on the mix, and it's nice talking to someone who isn't required by the law of families to be interested in me. Not like anybody could replace Lily, but I need to make some friends here.

"It's okay," I tell him. "You'll meet my father soon, and he'll probably be thrilled I'm talking to someone instead of sulking. Even though he warned me about strangers."

"Ah yes, strangers. Speaking of, can I interest you in some candy in my van?" Lucas snorts. "Well, in Lake Springs you won't be a stranger for too long. Everybody likes to be in everybody else's business. Small-town living at its finest." He points to the list in front of me. "So, in that spirit, I'm going to be nosy and ask you about the list you're making from the tape. Didn't you know what was on it?"

"Oh, well . . ." I debate whether or not to tell Lucas about the box. Since Lily isn't back for two more days, I've been itching to tell someone. "I found the cassette tape in a box buried in our backyard. It had all this random stuff in it and a picture of girls from back in 1989 and half of a best friend necklace and an apology note, and I'm just trying to piece it all together." It all comes out in one big flurry, like I've been holding it in for weeks instead of a single day.

Lucas leans in. "That is the coolest thing. It's like a mystery."

"Yeah, I guess." I hadn't thought of it like that, but that's exactly what it is. I'm like a detective trying to piece together all of the clues. Even though I have no idea how I'm going to do it. Or what any of the stuff in the box is. But still . . . I'm not going to pass up any kind of adventure.

Lucas clears his throat. He appears to be a little nervous. "So, like, do you need any help?"

I pause for a second. My plan was to do this on my own, but it would probably be better to have some help. Someone who knows the town. A bonus if that someone also knows where there's some really good ice cream.

I shrug. "Sure."

Maybe what could save this summer is having a partner in crime.

CHAPTER EIGHT

1989

"Good morning!"

"After an awesome evening," I reply to Jess as we wake up in my bedroom on Friday.

We spent last night going through our magazines and cutting out pictures of Jordan and Joey—and a few of the other New Kids: Donnie, Danny, and Jonathan—to include in our time capsule. Then after one too many Cherry Cokes, we took some silly pictures of us with the collage.

Dad went fishing with some friends for a couple of days, so Mom said I could have her over.

Things have returned to normal with us since the park. Maybe I was reading too much into nothing. If Jess was really sad about something, she'd tell me.

She kicks off her Snoopy sleeping bag and stretches. "And we have the sleepover at Amy's house tomorrow night. You're going to get so sick of me!"

"Never!" I reply, because there's like no way I could get bored with Jess. That's impossible. Even though I'm not as excited about the sleepover as she is. But at least we're doing it together.

She pats her stomach. "And now I am so ready for some Lucky Charms."

"I tripled-checked that we had some."

"Which is why you're my best friend."

What I don't mention was that Mom told me she felt guilty about feeding Jess something forbidden. But it's not like her parents don't know about it—we talk about sugar cereal all the time. Well, not *all the time*, but they know she eats it here. Jess's house is so much nicer than ours, but at least I can offer her better cereal.

We run downstairs in our pajamas to find the kitchen empty. Usually my mom is at the dining table in the morning, drinking coffee and reading the newspaper.

I reach on my tippy toes to get the bowls from the kitchen cabinet.

But then we hear a weird noise coming from the bathroom down the hallway.

"Is that . . . ?" Jess asks as her nose twitches.

I take a couple of steps closer and then back away when I hear the unmistakable sound of someone throwing up.

"Mom?" I call out, but take another step away.

I hate getting sick. I had the flu last winter, and I didn't make it to the bathroom in time and threw up all over the hallway carpet. Dad was mad, but he wasn't the one who had to clean it up. Mom did.

Ew, am I going to have to clean up after her?

"Are you okay?" I say a little louder.

The door cracks open, and I see Mom sitting on the floor. "Yeah, honey, I'm fine. Just a little under the weather."

"Should I call Dad?" I ask, but remember he's in the middle of some lake and there's no way to reach him. "Or Dr. Villa?"

"No! I'm fine. I'll be out soon. Don't worry about me. Fix breakfast for yourself and Jessica."

Well, now I don't have much of an appetite. As I round back into the kitchen, it seems that the disgustingness happening down the hallway hasn't dampened Jess's, though. She has poured herself an extra big bowl of cereal.

"Is she okay?"

I shrug. "She says she is."

"Do you want some?" Jess pushes the box to the center of the table.

"I guess . . ."

Mom walks back into the kitchen. Her face is pale, and she's grabbing her stomach.

"Are you sure you're okay?"

She nods. "Yes. I'm fine. Just haven't been feeling that well. Same thing happened yesterday, and I got better after a few minutes."

Jess kicks me under the table, and when I look across from her, she mouths something I don't understand.

What? I mouth back. I can't tell what she replies. All I know is that she doesn't want my mother to know, so we'll have to wait.

"Do you want some cereal, Mrs. Davis?" Jess offers.

Mom shakes her head. "No, I'm fine. And I'm starting to think that maybe we shouldn't have this stuff in the house either."

"No!" I protest, though I know Dad wouldn't let Mom totally ban Frosted Flakes anyway. It's like the only thing he and I agree on.

"Melissa, this stuff isn't good for you, and it's expensive. Or at least I'll start buying generic."

I look down at the table and shove a spoonful of cereal into my mouth. I get embarrassed when my parents talk about money, especially in front of Jess, since we don't have as much as the Millers. Jess's dad is a doctor, and her mother works on the board of the hospital. They go on nice family vacations and live in a big house with a huge basement with a giant TV. My dad works as a mechanic and often takes extra shifts. Mom waitresses during the school year at Kitchen Corner. She was going to work this summer, but Dad felt strongly about her being here when I'm home. "My mother was a homemaker, and I want the same thing for my daughter," I heard him say to Mom once.

It wasn't that I was eavesdropping; it's just sometimes my dad has very loud conversations with my mom. Well, maybe not conversations, because she doesn't say much in reply.

We don't have a lot of rules at home, but one is that Dad's word is law and we're not to argue.

It's not too hard, because I don't see him a lot, since he's up early for work and goes out with friends after. So I'm usually asleep when he comes home.

If he has a day off, I usually go to Jess's. He doesn't seem to mind. He thinks that I'm "too loud and silly." He's never understood me as much as Mom. And definitely not as much as Jess.

"So what did you two do last night?" Mom asks as she sits down and sips a glass of water.

My spirits immediately brighten. "Okay, are you ready for this?" I start.

"I'm ready." Mom leans forward in her seat.

"Okay, so *Big Bopper* had a quiz on which New Kid on the Block is your dream guy, and I got Joey—"

"And I got Jordan!" Jess finishes as we both squeal.

"Well, I guess that settles it," Mom says with a laugh. "I was a Paul girl myself."

Mom is always trying to tell me that she was also into a boy group when she was around my age, the Beatles. I've listened to some of their stuff, and it's good and all, but Paul McCartney is no Joey McIntyre.

Mom looks out as rain lightly beats against the window. "Looks like a dreary day. What do you guys have planned?"

"We're going to make a mix tape," Jess replies.

"The *best* mix tape!" I clarify.

It's a perfect rainy day activity: listening to the radio and waiting for the right song to come on.

"I'm sure it'll be great." Her focus is off to the distance.

"Are you really okay?" I ask.

"Yes." She says it, but I don't really believe her. Though if I just hurled, I'd also not be in a great mood, so I understand.

Jess slurps up the milk from her bowl, takes both our bowls to the sink, and washes them out. We both spend so much time at each other's houses, we pretty much make ourselves at home.

"Mrs. Davis, can we please be excused to go back upstairs to Mel's room?"

"Of course. And why don't I make some grilled cheese and tomato soup for lunch later?"

"Oh yes!"

Jess grabs my hand as we run up the steps. She closes the door and pulls me close to her.

"What is it?" I ask.

She whispers, "I think your mom might be pregnant!"

"WHAT?" I scream, right before Jess puts her hand over my mouth.

"It's the same thing that happened to my aunt Jenny when *she* was pregnant. She was sick almost every morning."

"That doesn't mean anything." That can't be right, even though the thought does get me excited.

"Morning sickness is a thing," Jess says. She's always reading nonfiction books about medicine so she can be a doctor just like her dad. (While I prefer The Baby-Sitter's Club). "It's also what happened to Mom before . . ." She trails off.

So Jess's mom had been pregnant a few times, but there were issues, and she was never able to carry a baby until it was ready to be born. That's why her parents decided to adopt.

A few years ago, Mrs. Miller was pregnant again. We were excited about it, but . . . Jess was worried her parents would love her less if they had a "real" baby of their own. I was over for dinner a few weeks after Mrs. Miller lost the baby. In the middle of dessert, Jess blurted out in tears, "It's all my fault. I thought I wanted a baby brother or sister, but then I was worried you'd give me away!" Her parents were so upset that she would ever feel less than their daughter just because she wasn't born to them. I realize now it was another time I had no idea what Jess was feeling inside.

It's so clear to me how much Jess's parents love her. I like to think it means even more that they would go through the long process to find her. To welcome her into their family before even holding her in their arms.

So Jess tilts her head at me. "What do you think?"

I don't know what to think. Even if Mom *was* pregnant, it would mean so much would change.

Jess plops down on my bed. "Aren't you excited?"

"I am, but we don't know anything for sure. So I don't want to get my hopes up," I reply. "Should I ask her?" I wonder what it would mean if I got a younger sibling. I asked for a little brother or sister—or puppy—for years, but Dad always said that the house was already too loud with just one kid.

Jess shakes her head. "No. Wait until she tells you. My mom didn't tell people until she was at a certain stage, and I've been told it's not polite to ask. But *when* she tells you, you have to promise to tell me!"

"I mean, of course, I'd tell you. *Duh*. I could never keep a secret from you."

"Same!" Jess grins as she turns on the radio. "Now let's get to the mix."

"What should be the first song?" I take out a tape, grateful for the distraction from the fact that my mom might be pregnant.

"Um, gee, let me think?" Jess gives me a look.

"I know, I know! New Kids!"

"They've mostly been playing 'I'll Be Loving You,' but I feel like we should start with a fun fast song."

"Right!" I turn up the volume. A car dealership commercial is currently playing. "I wish I had a dual cassette so we could just put 'The Right Stuff' on." Instead, I place the tape in my regular old boom box.

I have my finger on the record button and feel my heart start to beat faster. This is the problem with making a mix from the radio—we never know exactly what the next song will be. Sometimes the DJ will say something is coming up, but it'll be like ten songs later.

"Get ready!" Jess says as a few notes start to play.

"Ugh!" I pull my finger away as some boring rock song comes on. I don't even need to ask Jess if we're going to include it.

Two more songs come on that we deem unworthy.

"Coming up after the break, the latest song from Paula Abdul!" the DJ announces.

"Oh, fast song!" we say in unison. "*One, two, three, owe me a Coke!*" We both collapse on my floor giggling.

"I haven't heard the new one yet! I wonder if it's as good as 'Straight Up'?" Jess asks.

"You know 'Forever Your Girl' is my favorite."

It's one of the rare times we're in disagreement, but it doesn't really matter since both songs are totally awesome.

I kneel next to the boom box as a couple more commercials play.

Jess screams as the first few notes start, and I hit record. "*It's overcast and raining, but we've got the latest from Paula Abdul to brighten up your day. You're listening to Z104.*"

Ugh! I hate when the DJ talks over the song, but there's nothing we can do about it.

"It's kind of cool that whoever hears this will know which station we got it from."

"And, most importantly, what the weather is like," I say, which cracks Jess up.

After a few more giggles, Jess sits up straighter with a reflective look on her face. "You know what *is* cool? We have no idea what's going to be on this tape. It's kind of up to fate. It's like this summer. We know it's going to be great, but we don't know what will happen."

"It's a mystery!" I declare. Jess and I both love Nancy Drew novels.

"Yeah, but one part's not: we're solving it together."

CHAPTER NINE

It's a good day. About time!

"Lily!" I yell as her face fills the screen of my phone. Her light brown skin is tanner from being out in the sun at camp. It makes her green eyes stick out more. Her brown hair is pulled back in her signature high bun.

"Pey!" Lily hollers back. "I've missed you so much! SO MUCH!"

Lily throws her head back and lets out a big scream. She does everything big: laughs, hand gestures, pep talks. Seeing her now makes me miss her even more.

"Ahh! I've missed you!" I reply.

"Not as much as I've missed you!"

"And what about your dear old dad?" I hear Lily's dad's voice.

Lily rolls her eyes. She taps her phone so I can see her dad driving.

"Hi, Mr. Hernandez!" I call out.

"Hey there, Peyton! I've had my daughter back for all of two minutes, and she's already ignoring me."

Lily puts the screen back to her face. "I had to call you the second I got my phone back. It's like literally exploding with your texts, and I can't wait to look at every single one, but I needed to talk to you. I love, love, LOVE camp, but it wasn't the same without you . . . *you know*!"

"DON'T I!" we both scream and then burst out laughing.

"Tell me everything." I curl up on my bed, wanting to settle in so I can hear every single detail of the last week.

"Camp was awesome, and I was thinking of you all the time, like when they served the tater tot casserole. And then we had the dance, and our song came on, so I, of course, busted a move and did our dance, but nobody else knew the dance moves because of course they wouldn't, but I just closed my eyes and pretended you were there."

"Did you do this move?" I jump up and start pumping my fist in the air.

"You know it!" Lily joins me in our dance.

"Please tell me that Coach Megan still—"

"—wears the same smelly headband every day, ah yes she does! And then Shoshanna would—"

"—plug her nose behind her back!"

We both continue to laugh. It's like a part of me has returned. I don't have to explain myself to Lily. She just *knows*.

Lily's face falls. "But, seriously, Pey, it was hard. There were so many reminders of you everywhere, and now I'm going back home where you'll be missing."

"I know." Oh, how I know.

"Yeah, but you have this new house and new town, and I got so worried that you'd already forgotten about me."

"Are you serious?" I can't believe Lily would think that would ever happen. "That's like physically impossible, Lils. I'd never forget you."

I bite my lip.

"Oh, no, it's fine. I didn't mean to make you sad." Lily grimaces. "I want to hear about your move. How's the house? How's Jackson? Has he left his room at all? Have you met anybody? And have you told them that you already have a best friend so the position is filled?" She then holds up her right wrist to show the L+P bracelet.

I'm so glad Lily is also bursting with a zillion questions. "Where to start! Of course Jackson hasn't left his room. The move was awful. This town is so tiny. I don't know anybody. Well, I did meet this one kid at the library, but—"

Lily's face freezes on the screen.

"Lils?"

She says something, but it's muffled. Camp is located in the middle of farmland, so the reception probably isn't great.

"Lils?" I say again. I finally got my best friend back, and I don't want to lose her.

The screen goes blank. I hit redial, but she doesn't pick

up. I text her to call me when she gets home. I've waited a week; I can wait another two hours.

Then I realize that in two hours, I'm going to be at Lucas's for dinner.

I feel like crying. I miss Lily so much. All I want is to talk to my best friend.

But it's okay. It's going to be okay. It has to be.

I text her I'll call her when I get back from dinner. But there's this feeling in my gut that's gnawing at me. This is our new reality. Talking on the phone. Not being together. And it's even harder than I could imagine.

So this summer *could* get worse.

Cool.

Two hours later, we pull up in front of Lucas's house for dinner.

"Isn't this great?" Mom says with forced enthusiasm as we get out of the car.

"It is!" Dad replies with the same sickly sweet tone.

It's basically what they've been doing since they told me and Jackson we were moving: pretending that this is the Best! Idea! Ever!

Neither of us is buying it. Not then. Not now.

"Whatever." Jackson keeps his head down as he plays a game on his phone, his long brown bangs obscuring his face.

"Put that away," Mom orders Jackson.

"Why?" he asks. "You let me do it at home." Generally our dinners—on the rare occurrence the four of us sit down at the same table—are filled with silence as we all scroll on our phones. I'm totally guilty of it, except over the last week when Lily wasn't available.

"Well, we aren't home," Mom says as we make our way up to Lucas's. There's a dark wooden ramp with a slight incline leading to the door and a garden filled with plants and bright yellow daisies on either side. "Well, this is a lovely walkway, very different. And I love all these houses on this street and their flowery yards."

"So nice," Dad echoes, yet again.

"There's just so much space."

It takes everything I have to not scream at her *still* trying to sell us on the move. We're already here. The damage has been done.

"And we get to spend time together as a family." Mom puts her arm around me, but I shrug it off.

"Well, *three* of us have been around," I say not so quietly. Mom has basically been gone all week. Part of the argument for the move was that it would be better for the family, but what's the point if *the family* is never together?

"I'm so glad this dinner worked out," Dad says brightly to cut the tension.

It turned out Dad didn't mind me talking to strangers

when he picked me up from the library. He was even a tad horrifying when he saw Lucas's mom, his eyes lighting up. He did the whole shake-hands-and-fumble-over-how-excited-he-was-that-I-was-making-friends thing. As if I was some loner back home.

I'm only alone here because of them and this move.

So, yeah, Ms. Ryan ended up inviting us over for dinner, and here we are.

"So nice," Mom says again, like if she says it enough, all of our lives will stop being miserable. It'll be *just so nice*.

Whatever.

Okay, okay. Yes, it *is* nice that the four of us are spending time together. And as much as I want to be mad at Mom— she is the reason for the move, after all—it wasn't like we had many dinners together back in Minneapolis. Dad often worked late, and Mom taught night classes two days a week. During the weekends, Mom would be in her office grading papers while Jackson stayed in his room playing online and I'd be out with Lily.

Lily. I quickly glance at my phone and see she's gone through all of the seven thousand texts I had sent her the last week and replied to every single one.

"Peyton, you also need to put your phone away," Mom says.

I groan. Lily is finally around, and now I have to ignore her. Life is so not fair.

Mom rings the doorbell. We're greeted by a tall girl with big blue eyes and a cascade of honey-colored hair. She's a couple of years older than Jackson, probably sixteen. Upon seeing her, my weirdo brother stands up a bit straighter and pats down his unruly hair.

"Hello!" Mom greets her warmly. "We're the Howards! I'm Shannon; this is my husband, Kirk; and our children, Peyton and Jackson."

"Hey!" Jackson blurts out. He clears his throat. "Ah, what up . . . yo."

Oh, wow. *Wow*. My brother is so embarrassing when he has to talk to real people. I wish Mom would just let him be on his phone already.

The girl wisely ignores Jackson and opens the screen door. "Hey, I'm Zoe. Come on in. Mom's in the kitchen getting everything ready. I hope you like Italian. She gets a little carried away when we have guests."

Jackson laughs extra loud and ends up coughing. Way to play it cool, bro.

"Is that Peyton?" Lucas's voice drifts down the hallway.

"Hey!" I call out.

Lucas turns the corner and comes down the hallway . . . using a wheelchair.

"Um, hey," I repeat, trying to act normal.

When we were at the library, Lucas was sitting across from me. I didn't see him come in because I was so focused on the songs, and we left before he did. I had no idea he uses a wheelchair.

"Oh, hello!" Mom says, her voice a register higher than usual. "And how are you?"

She shoots me a look like I should've told her, but I didn't know either.

Lucas's mom comes down the hallway, a giant grin on her face. "Hello, Howards! I'm so happy to have you in our home." Another round of introductions are made.

"We brought this," Mom says as she hands Ms. Ryan a couple of pints of ice cream from Frannie's. I had mentioned that Lucas said he liked it, so we stopped by on our way here. Jackson's nose was practically up against the ice cream case, and he asked to try a zillion flavors before we decided on a carton of Summer Lovin', sweet cream swirled with rainbow cookies and sprinkles, and Taste of Joy, coconut with almonds and brownies.

"Do you, ah, like ice cream?" Jackson asks Zoe, who just stares at him, because *who doesn't like ice cream?*

Seriously, Jackson shouldn't ever be allowed to leave the house again.

"And please know, I'm very careful about food allergies," Ms. Ryan says. "So I tripled-checked to make sure nothing came from a facility that processes nuts, but I saved the labels if you'd like to inspect. And I have dishes that never come in contact with nuts."

"That's very thoughtful of you," Mom says with a smile.

It *is* very thoughtful. While my allergy isn't as severe as some, I bring my own food to sleepovers if there's any question to where something came from.

"Can I show Peyton my room?" Lucas blurts out.

Ms. Ryan laughs. She brushes her hand against his cheek. "Of course you can, sweetie."

"Come on!" Lucas says as he goes back down the hallway. It's then that I realize this house is only one floor.

Which makes sense.

I follow Lucas, and he enters into his bedroom. It's a pretty basic boy room—not that I've been in a lot of them, but I do have a brother. He has a brown desk with a laptop and a giant screen, along with a dresser against one wall and a bed on the other side. His closet is open partway, and I can see everything is hanging a lot lower than usual, probably so he can reach it.

"Cool room," I remark.

"Okay, so do you want to bring it up or should I?" Lucas raises his eyebrow at me.

"I brought all the stuff." I begin to take off my backpack, but Lucas stops me.

"I'm talking about the fact that you seem a bit flustered back there. Was it being inundated by my mother who can be *a lot*, or the fact that you didn't seem to realize I use a wheelchair?"

"Oh, I didn't know," I reply since I don't want to lie to him.

"Does it change anything with the box?"

"Why would it change anything?" I ask, confused. Yeah, I didn't realize Lucas uses a wheelchair, but I don't think that would make me feel any differently about having him help me. At least I hope it wouldn't have.

"Good." He gives me a satisfied nod. "And to answer the question I know you want to ask, but are worried will come across as rude, my mom and I were in a car accident three years ago. Drunk driver. My parents were already not doing that great, and they ended up getting a divorce shortly after, so Zoe and I live with my mom. And that's the truncated version of my life story. All good?"

"All good," I reply. I have a feeling Lucas has to give that speech a lot.

"Okay, so let's move on to the business at hand. Let me see the stuff." Lucas rubs his hands together excitedly.

"Yeah." I take off my backpack and show him the items that were in the box.

He studies the piece of paper with the letters that make no sense.

"So cool. This has to be some kind of code." He pushes up his glasses. "I can probably do some coding to break it."

"You know how to code?"

Lucas pulls his shoulders back. "Affirmative. I was

supposed to go to coding camp, but then my mom got cold feet at the last minute. She's a bit overprotective, if you haven't gathered that quite yet."

"Ugh, I'm sorry." I know a little something about not being able to go to camp because of mothers.

As I pull out my phone to show Lucas some pictures, I see I have three texts from Lily. I quickly reply back that I'll call her in a couple of hours, and then I open up my photos. "Here's what the box looks like."

Lucas reaches out to take my phone, but then his eyes get wide. "Whoa, whoa, *whoa*. I mean, I know I'm an impressive specimen and all, but slow down. We just met."

"What?" I look at him confused. He gestures toward my bracelet. The one that says L+P. Lily and Peyton.

It takes a second for me to register what he's implying.

"Oh, no, no, I—I—I mean . . . ," I stutter. "This is for my best friend, Lily. Lily with an 'L.'"

He tilts his head at me, a concerned expression on his face. "Are you sure? Because I know another name that for certain starts with 'L.'" Lucas points his thumbs toward his chest.

I open my mouth to reply, but nothing comes out because he's joking . . . right? I think he is. He has to be.

Then Lucas throws his head back and gives a huge snort. "Relax. I was being sarcastic. For future reference, it's a language I'm very well versed in."

"Oh, okay," I reply, feeling silly.

Lucas reaches out for my phone. "The photos?"

Oh, right. That. I quickly pass him my phone.

He scrolls through the photos. "Oh wow, Pac-Man stickers. Retro."

Lucas seems to know a lot about *retro*. His walls are covered with pictures of superheroes, but the characters look decades older than the ones I'm used to seeing in the movies. There's a chance the drawing of Superman over his desk is from the original comic books. Maybe he likes old things, which will be super helpful since history isn't my best subject.

"Melissa and Jessica!" Lucas says.

I turn around. "What?"

He holds up the photo of the top of the box. "They signed it."

Oh wow. We have names.

"Didn't you already know that?" He furrows his brow at my expression. "Oh, you're one of those people who doesn't know cursive."

"Hey!" I protest. "They didn't teach it at my school."

"Good luck with sixth grade at St. Mary's."

"Please tell me you're being sarcastic again."

"Afraid not."

I bite my lip hard. Here I was only worried about starting school without friends; I'd assumed I'd be up to speed . . .

Lucas can sense my panic. "It's okay, I can show you. Once we solve this thing."

"Thanks. So what do you think we should do next?"

Lucas has been working on this for only a few minutes and has gotten further than me. That should make me happy—we're getting somewhere!—but instead I feel a little useless.

He holds up the flat black plastic thingy. "Get this film developed."

"It's film? Of what?"

Lucas raises his eyebrows. "What do they teach you in the big city?"

Apparently not enough.

Lucas continues, "I'm just kidding. My grandfather taught me all about cameras. This one is super old—like they don't even make Disc cameras anymore. You know how we take pictures on our phones? Inside this case are pictures taken by a camera that uses film. So we have no idea what's on this disc, and the kind of cool thing is that the people who took it wouldn't know either. I mean, yes, of course they'd remember they took pictures on vacation or whatever, but they wouldn't be able to see the photos before they're developed. They didn't get to take a million different shots to get the perfect one."

I can only think about all the memories that would be lost or ruined.

"How do you know this stuff?"

Lucas shrugs. "Like I said, my grandfather. He used to be a repairman. He likes to take things apart and put them back together, to study them. I started joining him when I was little. I mean, what kid doesn't want to take apart a TV? Although I did draw the line when he tried to take apart my wheelchair while I was still in it." He laughs at the memory. "So, yeah, I just find it interesting to see how things evolve: TV, radios, computers . . . I code, but in a few years that'll probably be out of date and there'll be something new. What stays the same is that everything comes from something else. I like to understand the evolution."

"So I take it you know how to get this film developed."

He lifts an eyebrow at me. "I mean, that's what the internet is for." He wheels over to the desk and starts typing on his computer. "Back in the day, you could get film developed in a day or two. But this might take a little longer. I don't know much about disc film; it's usually in a canister."

Well, I do have all summer, after all. So no rush.

"Hello!" Lucas's mom comes into his room. "How is everything? Do either of you need anything? Peyton? Lucas? I can get you some water? Milk?"

"We're good, Mom," Lucas replies.

"Well, dinner in ten!" she says in her bright and sunny disposition before she heads out of his room.

"My mom means well enough, but as you can see, she can get a little overexcited about pretty much anything."

A thought hits me. "Wait a second, Lucas, did your mom grow up here? Maybe we should show her this stuff and she can help!"

"My mom was only six years old in 1989; she wouldn't have known Melissa or Jessica."

"But maybe we can ask her?"

"I'd really prefer we don't," Lucas replies. "Listen, I love my mom and all, but she rarely gives me any space. I don't know; this is just something I want to do without her."

That's exactly why I don't want my family to get involved with the box. I want to keep something for myself.

"Maybe we should post something online," I suggest. "Like . . . ah, we have some random junk?" I laugh at how completely unhelpful that would be.

"Oh! Oh! Me next! What if . . . we go door to door and see if we can find them?" Lucas says with a snort. *"Hello! Melissa? Jessica? We have your super-old mix tape!"*

"Or we could get a loudspeaker and play the mix loudly down every street—" I start.

"And then be like, does this song bring back memories?"

"I mean, that should *totally* work."

We both laugh, but it's pretty clear we have no idea what to do next.

A thought hits me. "Wait a second; at the library you said everybody is in everybody's business. Someone has to know these girls—women now, I guess. There has to be someone in this town—not your mom—who we could ask."

He tilts his head. "My grandparents pretty much know everything that's happening around here. We can start with them."

"Yes!" I say with a pump of my fist. Now we're getting somewhere. I hope.

Lucas holds out his hands. "Okay, okay, but I have to be

CHAPTER TEN

1989

"This is going to be so much fun!" Jess says as we walk up to Amy's house on Saturday night.

"So much fun . . ." I try to copy her enthusiasm. I know we'll have a good time. We've had sleepovers with other people before.

I don't know why I'm so nervous. I'm being silly. I'm going to have fun tonight. It's a sleepover, not a dentist appointment.

"Hi!" Amy greets us at the front door. She's already wearing her pajamas, a white nightgown with blue ribbons and a matching bathrobe. It's so pretty that I'm regretting packing my ratty old Garfield nightshirt. "I'm so glad you guys are here! Autumn and Kristi are in the kitchen fawning over Mike." Amy sticks her tongue out in disgust.

Amy's older brother is going to be a freshman next year, and most of the girls in our school have a crush on him. He's blond with curly hair and blue eyes, just like Amy. Some people think he looks like a young blond Patrick Swayze, but I don't really get the big deal. He's no Joey McIntyre. But then again, who is? *Swoon.*

"Hey, guys!" Jess says as we walk into the kitchen.

Mike is tossing around a basketball as Autumn and Kristi gaze at him in wonder.

"What do you nerds have going on tonight?" he asks.

They laugh in response. Amy takes the ball away from him. "We're having a sleepover, and no boys are allowed."

"*You* can stop by." Kristi giggles before Amy tells him that he and his friends are under *no circumstance* allowed in the basement.

Amy's mom walks into the kitchen. "Michael, stop bothering your sister and her friends." Mike pushes off the counter and gives us a nod of his chin before walking out.

Mrs. Campbell shakes her head. "So, girls, Pizza Hut is on its way, and we rented *Princess Bride.*" She takes a VHS case out of a plastic Family Video bag.

"Yes!" Amy and Jess exclaim at the same time.

"*One, two, three, owe me a Coke!*" Jess says to Amy.

Amy goes over to the refrigerator and hands Jess a Coke.

"Nice!" Jess replies as she pops open the can. "I don't think Mel has ever actually given me a Coke, and we do jinx *a lot.*"

Amy and Jess smile as they drink their soda while I stand

there, unsure of where I fit into all of this. I don't like feeling as if I don't belong somewhere. It's never usually a problem when Jess and I are together, but . . .

"Let's go!" Amy opens the door to the basement, and we all file downstairs.

The Campbells' basement is bigger than my whole house. There's a large couch on one end, and a huge TV. *Huge*, like thirty inches. Everybody starts laying out their sleeping bags on the floor. I make sure mine is next to Jess's. We always stay awake at sleepovers and whisper to each other after everybody else has gone to sleep.

"You don't really mean 'no boys allowed'?" Kristi asks as she runs her fingers through her stick-straight dark hair. She has the longest hair in the entire school. It's nearly to her waist, and she always wears it down to show it off.

Amy groans. "Yes. Especially if that boy is my brother."

Autumn sits cross-legged on the floor. "Okay, but is he really seeing Heather O'Connor? Like, are they dating?"

Both Kristi and Autumn giggle excitedly. But I don't care who Michael Campbell is dating.

"You guys are so boy crazy," Amy says with a laugh. "But these are the only boys I care about!" She goes to the coffee table and holds up the copy of *Teen Beat* that I got the other day at Book World, the one with New Kids on the cover.

"Yes!" Jess calls out.

"*Oh, oh, oh-oh-oh!*" Amy starts singing, doing the leg

shuffle dance from the "The Right Stuff" video. Jess joins her, but I stay frozen on my sleeping bag. I always mess up that part; I swear I have two left feet.

"Come on, Mel!" Jess calls to me, but she knows I get embarrassed that I can't do it right, so she doesn't push too hard.

Autumn joins them, while Kristi stays next to me. "I'm not really into them," she says, blowing a big bubble with her gum. "I mean, they're okay. I like that one song. Not this one, the slow one." Okay, I don't agree with Kristi about New Kids, but I'm glad I'm not the only one who isn't dancing.

It does look like Jess and Amy are having a blast. "Joey is my favorite!" Amy declares, and I feel jealousy bubbling up as I watch her dancing with *my* best friend and talking about *my* crush.

Yeah, okay, like I know a million other girls are in love with Joey McIntyre—because how could they not be?—but still.

But Jess has my back. "You can't marry Joey because Mel is marrying Joey," she says. She shuffle dances over and then drops down to sit right next to me.

As she throws her arm around me, I feel a little bit better.

"You can have Joey. I also think Corey Haim is so dreamy." Amy falls down on her sleeping bag. "Why can't the boys in Lake Springs be like the ones in *Teen Beat*?"

"*Your brother* is dreamy," Kristi replies as she and Autumn break down in giggles.

"Gross!" Amy throws her pillow at them. "My brother is disgusting and rude and smelly . . ."

"And cute with his dimples!" Autumn pretends to collapse on her sleeping bag.

"You guys are hopeless!" Amy takes out a large plastic bag and places it in front of her. "Okay, so! Yesterday at parks and rec, I came up with the best idea." She pulls out threads in different colors and places them in front of us. "Friendship bracelets! I was thinking we could do matching ones and wear them this summer."

"That sounds great!" Autumn says, and everybody else agrees. One by one they start grabbing strings. And . . . I guess that would be fine to do. I can't help but reach up to touch the best friend necklace that Jess and I both wear. It's not like Amy's saying we're all best friends. It's not a *best friend*ship bracelet.

Amy fans out the strings to show us what to do, suggesting a pattern of purple, pink, and white.

Jess leans in to me. "We should put a friendship bracelet in our time capsule!"

I perk up. The time capsule! Yes, that would be a great idea. It could be a fun thing for someone to find someday in the future.

I wonder if it'll be like *The Jetsons* with flying cars and robot maids.

Amy looks over. "Are you talking about the school's time capsule?"

"No, it's nothing," I reply quickly.

She raises her eyebrow at us. "You guys and your secrets." Amy shakes her head as she ties a knot.

Um, yeah, we have secrets. It's one of the benefits of having a best friend: having someone to confide in.

But then Jess blurts, "Mel and I are doing our own time capsule this summer!"

I feel sick to my stomach. I thought our time capsule was something Jess and I were doing, just the two of us. Not with a big group. It's supposed to be about our summer. Jess and me.

"What are you putting in it?"

"You should totally include a picture of the New Kids!"

"And Mike!"

"Gross!"

The basement is so flooded with suggestions and questions about the time capsule that I start to hear buzzing instead of voices. I feel like our amazing, fun idea is slipping away from me and maybe so is Jess. That our summer is going to be filled with Amy and Kristi and Autumn and their ideas.

I stand up on unsteady feet. "I have to use the bathroom," I say, but I don't think anybody hears me.

I walk up the stairs and see Amy's parents at the kitchen table. "Pizza should be here soon!" her mom says as I walk to the powder room off the kitchen.

I look in the mirror, trying to tell myself not to get upset.

Not to get threatened by having other people involved in our plans. But I can't help it.

I don't have a fancy house or fancy parents. I don't really have a lot, but what I do have means a lot to me, especially Jess. She makes me feel special. She makes me feel safe.

There's a knock on the door, and Jess comes in. The room is tiny, but she squeezes in next to me.

She bites her bottom lip, and instantly I know that she regrets bringing it up. "I'm so sorry. I wasn't thinking. The time capsule is just between us, okay?"

I nod, fighting the tears that are sprouting up in my eyes.

Jess pulls out her necklace. "Hey, you and me. Best friends." She takes my half and puts them together. "Forever."

"Forever," I reply back.

CHAPTER ELEVEN

Not sure what I was more naive about: that it would be easy to find two girls who lived in this town in 1989 or that once Lily got back from camp, everything would return to normal.

It's been forty-eight hours since she's been home. But we can't seem to actually talk. It's only been texts. Which are fine and all, but I need to see her face.

My chest feels heavy as I wait for her to FaceTime me. It shouldn't be too much to ask to have a conversation with my best friend, but that's easier said than done. We finally found a time that works for us both. I can't wait to tell Lily all about the box and Lucas.

I feel tears start to burn behind my eyes. I don't want Lily to see me like this, like I'm some needy kid. But I remember she's seen me at my worst: crying after we lost the last game of the season because I missed a penalty kick, humiliated after Braeden Hamilton made fun of me when I got braces, and pretty much every other ordeal that's part of being a girl in middle school.

I see Lily's face fill my phone screen, and the rest of my doubts fade away.

"Ah, hi!" I scream.

"Oh my goodness, finally!" Lily says, leaning back on her gingham duvet cover. I've spent so much of my life lying next to her, trading secrets on that bed. "I'm so sorry, Pey. Things got crazy when I got back from camp. Plus, I'm in denial that we have to set up phone dates like it's the Middle Ages. I need you here."

That's all I want, too.

"So tell me everything. Who is this Lucas that you texted me about? Is he cute?" Lily wiggles her eyebrows.

"It's not like that," I reply. "He's basically the only person I know. And he's helping me with a project!"

I didn't text Lily about the box because I wanted to *talk* to her. "You're not going to believe this, but I found a box buried in the backyard."

Lily sticks her tongue out. "Gross. Please tell me you didn't open it."

"I did—"

"Peyton!" she screams as she closes her eyes and shakes her head. "No! Ew!"

"Wait, it's actually pretty cool. It's from—"

Lily flips her phone around so I'm seeing the door to her

room. "No, I don't want to hear about some dead animal! Don't you remember when we buried Chewie in the court-yard of our building?"

Of course I remember. Chewie was Lily's pet guinea pig who died last year. I brought flowers for Lily and one single rose to put where we buried him.

"It's a time capsule!" I finally shout over her "ewwws" so she'll listen to me.

Lily flips the phone back around. "A what?"

"At least that's what I think it is. It's this box filled with all this stuff from 1989, and I just made this playlist from something called a cassette tape—"

"What are you even talking about? It's like I leave for a week and you're speaking some weird code. Who are you?"

"What? I'm still the same person." I try to keep it light, but my throat hurts.

Lily tilts her head and furrows her brow. "Oh, Pey, I'm just teasing. I'm sorry."

Lily could see by whatever look that's on my face that I'm getting upset. We just know this stuff about each other. Last summer she could tell when I was about to come down with a cold before *I* even knew. "You're a lot quieter, and you look pale—I think you're getting sick," she had said to me as she placed her hand against my forehead, a worried look on her face. Now, she can't reach out with her hand. All we have is our phones. But she's still there.

"No, it's okay."

There's an awkward pause between us. This wasn't how I pictured our conversation would go.

Honestly, I didn't think this was how my summer would go either. We didn't find out about the move until a few weeks ago when Mom was given the opportunity to head up the English Department. It was her dream job and a big promotion for her. Before I could wrap my mind around what that meant for me, we were busy packing up our things.

Mom never even asked Jackson or me what we thought. Probably because she knew what my answer would be.

"Okay, so tell me all about this box and what's in it." Lily gives me a hopeful smile.

I instantly feel better. We can make this work.

"I listened to this cassette tape at the library; that's where I met Lucas. It has all these songs—"

There's a pinging sound. Lily's eyes glance toward the top of the screen, and she bursts out laughing. "Oh my gosh. So sorry, Pey, but I'm on this group chat with the girls from camp."

And just like that my hopeful feeling fades.

The girls from camp. That used to include me.

I kept arguing that I should still be allowed to go to camp, but no. There was too much going on with the move. It didn't matter what I wanted. I did what I was told.

"Tell them I say hi!" I say, trying to make sure that I'm

still part of that world. "And how's Shoshanna?" Shoshanna has been going to the same camp as Lily and me for forever. She lives in Wisconsin, so we can't hang out during the school year, but we'd occasionally video chat while watching movies.

She's so fun. Everybody in my old life was amazing.

Well, except for Braeden Hamilton. Because boys are the worst. I can't believe the only kid my age I've met here so far is a boy. And a pretty nerdy one at that.

Nope! Focus on the positive! I'm talking to Lily!

I nod along as Lily fills me in on camp.

"Shosh is *ah*-mazing. She grew like eight feet." Lily reaches her hand up high above her head. "No joke. She towers over everybody, so she has incredible speed. No one can catch up with her on the field. Oh, one night Mariah and Callie—"

"Who's Callie?"

Lily's jaw drops. "I can't even believe Callie wasn't there last year. You'd love her. She is *hi*-larious. I feel like I've known her my entire life."

A pang of jealousy erupts in my gut, as *I* actually *have* known Lily her entire life. We grew up in the same apartment building. I don't ever remember a time when Lily wasn't in mine.

Until now.

"Well, Callie lives just a half hour away, so the whole

Minny crew are totally going to do monthly sleepovers. It's going to be *ah*-mazing!"

It does sound pretty cool, but it also makes me incredibly envious. I'm surprised I'm not turning green. The Not-So-Incredible Peyton.

"What's with all the *ah*-mazing and *hi*-larious?" I ask. Lily never spoke with weird emphasis on words before.

"It's just a camp thing," she replies with a laugh. "Oh! Look at our team shirts!"

She holds out her phone and angles it so I can see the blue T-shirt she's wearing. It has the logo of the camp and signatures of all the campers. Lily and I would always sign our names next to each other and draw a bubble around them so we'd be together. She zooms in so I can see her signature—"Lily" written in all caps with a soccer ball for the dot in the "i"—and the rest of our friends, and now Callie. They wrote, "Team Amazing!"

They're in one big bubble now with me nowhere to be found.

"That's cool," I force out.

I had thought that talking to Lily would make everything better, but instead it's a reminder of all I'm missing out on.

"But camp wasn't the same without you!" Lily adds, using her BFF sixth sense that I'm bummed out. "Seriously, I think I said about four gazillion times a day that Peyton would've loved something or thought of something we had done. I don't have to talk about camp if it makes you sad."

"It's okay," I reply because I don't want Lily to feel like she can't talk to me. Best friends tell each other everything. "It sounds . . . *ah*-mazing." I try it out on my tongue, but it just feels wrong.

All of this feels wrong.

There's another pinging noise, and Lily's eyes flicker to the top of her screen again. "No way, Brigid"—Brigid is yet another person I don't know, but someone my best friend has new memories with—"has this crush and—" Another text comes in, and she squeals in a very non-Lily way.

Sure, we get excited about stuff, but we've never been those girls who freak out over things like boys or crushes. We jumped around and lost our minds when the US Women's National Team won the World Cup (*again*).

"Should I let you go?" I ask, since now I feel like I'm keeping Lily from something.

"No, of course not!" Lily says, but her attention keeps shifting to the top of her phone instead of staying on her best friend.

"I'm going to send you the mix. It's got some good songs to dance around to!" I say brightly. I want to remind her that I can be fun, too. It doesn't matter that I'm so far away.

"Huh?" Lily says. Her focus is on the texts, but then she

snaps back to me. "Sorry, Pey. Yes, the mix! I can't wait to listen to it. Ah . . ." Her attention drifts away again. "Sorry, sorry! There's just all these texts coming in and lots going on, and I don't want to miss anything. You know how camp withdrawal can be."

I take in a sharp breath. I feel like the wind has been knocked out of me. I have spent the last several *years* sharing every moment with Lily. How could she compare camp withdrawal to withdrawal from *me*?

Lily notices the look on my face. "Oh, I mean . . . I miss you so much, Pey!"

All I've been doing since Lily left for camp is miss her. I couldn't wait for her to come back. For something in my life to return to normal.

But it doesn't really feel like she misses *me* that much. And now there's this sick feeling in my gut that maybe things with Lily will never be normal again. How can they when we're so far apart?

There's another ping on Lily's end. She glances up at the top of her screen, and her eyes get wide.

"So, ah, I'll let you go," I say, because I know I'm about ready to cry. It'll be the first time in my new bedroom.

I have a feeling it won't be the last.

"No, Peyton. I want to talk to you," she says, but all I can hear is the constant pinging coming from her phone.

"Yeah, it's totally okay." Even though it isn't. None of this is okay. "I'll talk to you later." I force myself to smile even though I'm breaking down inside.

Lily beams back at me. "You know you're the best, Pey! Miss you, love you!"

"Miss you—" But I stop when the screen goes blank.

"If you think 1989 is retro, wait until you see the inside of my grandparents' house," Lucas says to me the next afternoon. "They have all this old stuff from their own grandparents, including—I kid you not—a coffee grinder where you had to use your actual hand to grind coffee. Can you imagine? Talk about not making anything easy *back in the day*."

Lucas's mom is driving us over in her van, which is super cool. The door on Lucas's side lifts up instead of sliding to the side, and there's this little ramp that comes down so he can easily get in and out.

"You kids are so spoiled," she replies with a laugh. "And I'll have you know that 1989 was not that long ago."

"Please, I bet you didn't even have running water."

"I'm going to ignore that comment, mister." She looks at me in the rearview mirror. "Why are you so interested in 1989?"

"I found this picture from—" I stop myself when I realize Lucas is glaring at me.

But it's too late.

"What picture? Who's in it? Do you need me to look at it? If it's from back then, maybe I can help?" She starts rattling off questions.

I see what Lucas meant about her being overly involved.

"Oh, nothing. It's just an old piece of junk I found while cleaning out the house," I say, hoping to not make Lucas mad, and also trying to get his mom to not insert herself.

"Can I see it? Maybe I know the people? Can you tell where the picture was taken? How many people are in it?"

"Please give her the photo before she spontaneously combusts," Lucas says with a frown.

She looks at the photo while we're at a stop sign, and her hopeful expression softens. "Oh, I don't know these girls."

"Told you," Lucas says to me with his eyes slit.

"It's okay, it's really not a big deal." I try to downplay it.

"Are you sure? I can post something online! I can ask around! This could be so much fun!" His mom does a little clap before handing me back the photo.

Wow, so Lucas was right in not mentioning it to her. That was . . . *a lot*.

"It's nothing, Mom," Lucas says with a groan.

"But, Lucas, I can help—"

"I want to do this on my own." He glances at me. "I mean, it's something that Peyton and I can do on our own."

She furrows her brow. "But is this why you're going

to your grandparents'? It's okay for them to help you, but not me?"

I cringe because she has a point.

Lucas sighs. "I have a couple questions for them, that's it. And well . . ."

"Well, *what*?" There's a hardness in his mom's voice.

Lucas lets out a loud groan. "You have to start letting me do some things without you hovering. You have to trust me!"

Ms. Ryan pulls the van over and turns her body around. "I do trust you!"

"You don't! You don't think I can handle two minutes by myself."

"It's not that, Lucas—"

"It is. You have to let me do this on my own. *Please.*"

I sink down in my car seat in an attempt to disappear.

Ms. Ryan grips the steering wheel tightly and maneuvers the van back onto the street. "Fine. I won't get involved."

Lucas replies by folding his arms. I continue to pretend like I'm somewhere else.

I jump as my phone buzzes. It's Lily. Phew. Not that I need any excuse to talk to her, but it'll help me escape the coldness between Lucas and his mom.

"We're here!" Lucas says, thankfully cutting through the tension. He sees me staring down at my phone. "It's okay. We need a minute."

I FaceTime Lily back. "Hey!" I say as I walk to the sidewalk.

"Hey, you! I guess the fourteenth time's the charm!" She laughs. Our timing has continued to be off.

Lily notices I'm outside. "Where are you?"

"Oh, I'm with Lucas! We're going to see if his grandparents know the girls from the picture."

Lily looks confused. "What picture?"

"You know, from the box."

"Right!" She smacks her forehead. "Yeah, that's cool and everything."

There's something off in her voice. I know that me trying to get some answers from a box that was buried over thirty years ago isn't quite the same as competing in soccer tournaments, but it's kind of the only thing I have going on right now. And I do think it's cool.

"Yeah, it is!" I reply.

She nods at me. I nod back at her.

We've never been this off before.

"Everything good with you?" I ask.

"Ah, yeah . . . Do you need to go?"

"Oh, um . . ." I look over and see that Lucas is out of the van and making his way to me.

I'm torn. I don't want to be rude to him, but I feel like I haven't spoken to Lily in weeks, even though it was actually just twenty-two hours ago. (And yes, I'm counting.)

"Hey, can I call you later when I get home?"

Lily frowns. "I'm meeting up with Callie and the crew at *the Mall*."

"Aw, man." I try to not let the jealousy seep into my voice.

"Wish you were here."

"Me, too."

Lily and I would always have the best time running around the behemoth that is the Mall of America. We usually go play mini golf or go on the roller coaster. Or walk around the ginormous LEGO Store.

"Well, maybe tomorrow then," Lily says with a grimace. "Have fun with Lucas."

The way she says Lucas's name makes me think that maybe she's also a little envious I have someone new.

"Okay," I reply. I feel sad when we hang up. We're just not in sync anymore.

"So was that the infamous other L in your life?" Lucas says with a crooked grin.

"Yeah, that's Lily!" I try to say brightly, but it's forced. I want to go back to when everything was natural for me, especially things with Lily.

"Cool." Lucas tilts his head like he's sensing something I'm not saying. I look away because I don't want to think about Lily right now. About how I can't help but feel that she's slipping away.

"So this is your grandparents'?" I begin to make my way up the walkway.

Lucas follows me. "You know, there's a mall about thirty minutes away. It doesn't have an amusement park, but it's still pretty cool."

"Oh, good to know." I try to sound enthusiastic, but know Lucas isn't buying it.

"Hey, even if they don't know anything, Grandma June makes one mouthwatering chocolate chip cookie."

I give him a smile. I can't really eat homemade treats from other people due to the possibility of cross-contamination with my peanut allergy, but all I want right now is some answers. To feel like one thing in my life is moving forward, not backward.

Lucas's mom being *a lot* can be a good thing.

I take a huge bite of probably the gooiest chocolate chip cookie in the history of chocolate chip cookies.

"Holly made sure I used specific brands and even brought over a mixing bowl and baking sheet for me to use," Lucas's grandma June begins to explain. "She wanted me to be extra careful with your allergy."

"Thanks!" I wipe the chocolate from my hands, even though I want to shove my fingers into my mouth to enjoy every bite. It's rare that someone goes through all the trouble, so I want to make sure her work wasn't in vain. You know, I'm all about being thoughtful. I take a second still-warm cookie.

"Let's see what you got here." Lucas's grandfather sits across from us at the table. He has the same pale green eyes as Lucas, with a massive amount of white hair on top of his head. He puts on his glasses as Lucas hands him the photo of Melissa and Jessica. "Well, would you look at that . . ."

I sit up straighter.

He shows his wife the photo. "Remember when the kids used to wear their hair all big and curly?" He shakes his head.

"Do you know them?" Lucas asks. "They'd be in their forties now."

"Your mother didn't know them?" Grandma June asks.

Lucas shakes his head.

"Were there a lot of Asian families in Lake Springs thirty years ago?" I ask.

Grandpa Jack leans back in his chair. "There were the Lings."

"They moved here when Holly was in high school. That was over a decade later," Grandma June replies. She wipes her hand on her apron and sits down at the kitchen table with us.

"That's right," Grandpa Jack replies. "You know, I saw Joseph at the grocery store the other day. He might have an old DVD player for me to fix. He was going to buy a new one since he has all these DVDs for the grandkids to watch, but I told him there was no sense in buying a new one when I could easily—"

"Focus!" Lucas says with a shake of his head. "Can we get back to the photo?"

"Right, right." His grandfather squints at it.

This was hopeless.

"Hey, Juney, didn't that dentist over there on Oak have an adopted daughter from China?"

Or . . . maybe not so hopeless. Could one of the girls have been adopted? And would that help at all in finding her?

Grandma June shakes her head. "No, you're thinking of that doctor, I think. The one that we went to see when Aaron had his tonsils removed."

"I thought Dr. Harkins removed Aaron's tonsils, and his children are much older."

"You're thinking of, oh what's his name . . . ?" Grandma June snaps her fingers as if the answer will suddenly appear.

This goes on for, no kidding, nearly a half an hour. In that time I get a lot of information about the town—the new hospital that opened up five years ago, the neighbors and their loud dog, that Lucas's uncle Aaron had to get his tonsils removed twice, which I didn't think was humanly possible. What we don't find out is any new information about Melissa and Jessica.

I take comfort by eating yet another chocolate chip cookie.

"Can you ask around?" Lucas takes a picture of the old photo on his grandfather's phone. "Anybody who was around then?"

Lucas's grandma perks up. "Oh, that reminds me. I have to make some brownies for the Weismans' potluck!"

He mouths *sorry* to me as he puts the photo away, but, hey, it was worth asking. Better than randomly knocking on doors (because I'm sure my parents would be totally fine with that).

"Oh, Lucas, I got a new gadget that we can play around with." His grandfather gets up to go to the garage as his grandmother picks up the home phone, which has rung no less than five times while we've been here. Lucas's grandparents sure know a lot of people in this town, just not the two we're trying to find.

"Hello, hello!" a voice calls out. A woman with dirty blond pulled-back hair and a large birthmark on the corner of her forehead enters the kitchen.

"Hey, Aunt Amy!" Lucas says as he gives her a salute. "This is my friend, Peyton. Peyton, this is my aunt Amy. She's married to my uncle."

"Hey there, squirt." Amy ruffles Lucas's hair. "Nice to meet you, Peyton. What are you guys up to?"

"Just getting the history of Lake Springs one long and disjointed story at a time."

Amy picks up a cookie. "Is there any other way?" She gives him a wink before Grandma June calls her over to talk about a recipe.

"So that's that, I guess," I say, defeated.

Now what?

My phone beeps. I pick up, expecting the text to be from Lily, but it's from my mom.

I stare at my phone, trying to figure out what she was thinking.

My mother has set up a playdate for me. What am I, five?

"What is it?" Lucas asks.

"My mom's new work friend has a daughter my age, and I guess I'm going over there tomorrow."

Yet another thing I wasn't asked about. Just told.

Not that I don't want to make more friends, but it would be nice to be included on decisions that affect me.

Lucas snorts. "What are you, five?"

I give him a shocked look.

"What?"

"Nothing, it's just I thought the exact same thing."

"Oh." Lucas taps his head and then points to me. "The mind meld has begun. Quick: What am I thinking right now?"

That this whole thing is pointless. Instead I reply, "That we clearly haven't had enough sugar and should go to Frannie's."

"Yes!" Lucas pumps his fist in the air. "I'll text my mom that we're ready. I told you it was the best."

It really was. One mouthful of their ice cream and I was in heaven. I guess that's one thing Lake Springs has that Minneapolis doesn't.

"Did your mom say who you're hanging out with?" he asks.

I look at her message. "Madison Kandel."

Lucas cringes. "Yikes."

"What?"

He shakes his head. "Nothing, but just good luck."

Good luck?

With my track record lately, I figure I'm due for some right now.

"Just ten more minutes," Dad texts me for the third time in a row. "Promise," he throws in at the end. I'm not holding my breath.

I sit on the swing on our front porch as I wait for him to be done with another "important business call." There are never any "casual" or "time-wasting" calls. Everything is just *so important*.

But so is being on time for meeting potential new friends.

I swing nervously as I think about meeting Madison. All Lucas would say about her is that she's "*that kind of girl.*"

Whatever that means. It doesn't seem good.

But it did make me stress over what I would wear, and *I've* never been *that girl*. Usually when I'm with Lily, we have on shorts and T-shirts. Sometimes we'll rock our US women's soccer jerseys—I have both Megan Rapinoe and Alex Morgan. Our hair is up to avoid getting it in our faces, and we don't really wear makeup. It'll just get sweated off when we're running around the field.

I want to make a good impression and all, but I still want to be me. So I'm wearing jean shorts and my favorite red tank top with lace straps. Lily has the same in blue.

"Sorry!" Dad comes out the door.

I don't reply because I'm getting used to his empty excuses and promises.

"Let's go!" he says cheerily before we drive the whole fourteen blocks to Madison's house.

"I don't see why I couldn't have biked."

"P, we've had this talk. Even though it's a small town, doesn't mean it's completely safe. Once we know the town—and people—more, maybe you can bike, but let's just wait and see. Okay?"

Not like I have much of a choice.

Dad pulls up to Madison's house. It looks very similar to the rest of the houses on this block: two stories with a two-car garage. A stone and wood outside. A driveway with a basketball hoop, and a fenced-in backyard.

"Rumor has it, she has a pool," Dad says with a wink as I get out of the car. He follows behind me. "Your mother asked me to make sure you get settled in okay."

"Then why isn't she here?" I say it with an attitude that isn't usually tolerated in our house, but I can't help it.

"Okay, P." Dad pulls me aside. "I know this has been hard on you, but it hasn't been easy on any of us, especially your mother. She's got a huge promotion and has a lot of catching up to do. Things will get back to normal soon."

I give him a "yeah right" look. When Mom is teaching, it's all classes and office hours and faculty meetings and grading papers.

"Please don't tell me you're already sick of your old man being around!" He tries to make light of the situation.

I reply by walking up to the front door. I just want to get inside and meet Madison and her friends and see if there's a chance I can get settled into Lake Springs.

The door's opened by a girl with shiny, wavy dark brown hair. It's pulled back in a headband. She's wearing a floral T-shirt and a denim skirt. Behind her are three other girls dressed nearly identically. One is white with chin-length blond hair, one has light brown skin and curly brown hair, and one is Asian, with black hair in a neat ponytail.

"You must be Peyton," Madison says. She has a smile on her lips, but her eyes scan my outfit.

I'm totally being judged right now. My legs start bouncing around like they do when I get nervous. Lily used to say she could tell when it was a game day from the amount my knees would move during lunch.

"Hey, Madison, I'm Peyton's dad." My dad inserts himself. "Thanks for having her over. She can text me when she's ready to be picked up."

Madison's mom approaches and talks to him. They joke about being faculty spouses while Madison guides me into a large living room.

She plops down on the couch and puts her feet up. I'm not really sure what to do, so I sit in the empty space on the couch next to the other white girl.

"Hey, I'm Isabel, but my friends call me Izzy," she says.

"Hey, Izzy," I reply.

Madison laughs, but it doesn't have much joy in it. "We didn't say *you* were friends with her yet." She blinks at me like she's innocent, though I have a feeling I know the *type* Lucas was referring to. The sour candy wrapped in pretty paper.

"She's just joking," the curly-haired girl replies. "I'm Patrice, and that's what everybody calls me, so we're cool."

"Peyton," I say, even though they already know that.

"And I'm Skylar," the Asian girl gives me a warm smile.

"Hey, it's great to meet everybody." Maybe things in Lake Springs will be okay after all. "Do you all go to St. Mary's?"

"Yes and it's been forever since we've had anybody new in our grade," Izzy replies. "You're from Minneapolis, right? I'm sure Lake Springs is so different."

"Yeah, it's taking some getting used to," I admit.

"We moved to Lake Springs when I was six," Skylar says. "It took my older brother, who was ten, a bit to adjust, but he loves it here now. It just took some time."

Yeah, I feel like it's going to take me *a lot* of time.

"I can't imagine moving away from my friends," Patrice adds. "Although every once in a while I'd think I'd love to escape to a big city . . . or any kind of city, really."

"Did you like living in Minneapolis?" Izzy asks.

"Oh, yeah. I really like living there. Or I guess *liked*." I feel my throat catch, that I have to talk about that part of my life in the past tense.

Will it ever come to a point where I have to say Lily *was* my best friend?

"What did you guys do there?" Izzy asks.

"Oh my God, Isabel," Madison says with a roll of her eyes. "She lived a few hours away, not in another country."

"Oh, sorry," Izzy replies in a soft voice.

"No, it's cool." I give her a smile. It's nice that she's interested in me. I should probably find out more about them. "Do any of you play soccer?"

"Soccer?" Madison scrunches her nose.

"Yeah. I'm part—*was* part of an awesome soccer team. There doesn't seem to be a summer league here. Do you know if there's one during the school year?" My internet research came back with zero in terms of a soccer league I could join.

"Um, no," Madison says with a sniff.

"There's a boys' team," Patrice offers. "I think they play in the spring."

"Oh, well, I guess that's better than nothing."

Madison actually shudders. "You're not seriously going to join the boys' team?"

I shrug. "If that's the only option. Not like they'd be able to keep up with me," I brag because it's true.

Last summer we'd had it with the boys trash-talking our team. They kept saying that we only won regionals because our competition isn't as hard as theirs. So Lily told them to put their money where their mouth is. We played a scrimmage. Losers had to buy the winners pizza.

Let's just say that victory had never tasted so delicious.

"That's pretty awesome," Patrice says with an impressed nod. "I wanted to play so badly after watching the women's soccer team win."

"Aren't they amazing?" I say. "And I can teach you some moves."

"Really?" Her big brown eyes get wide. "That would be awesome."

"Oh, I want to learn, too," Skylar replies with an enthusiastic clap.

Maybe making friends here won't be so hard.

Madison clears her throat. "I mean, sure, you could run around, or we could hang by the pool. Maybe ask Eliot over."

The four girls coo and start talking excitedly about people I don't know. And just like that, I'm back to being on the outside.

I wonder if what Lucas meant was Madison is the kind of girl who doesn't like the attention off her. The type that has to be in charge.

Madison keeps going on about some birthday party with people I don't know. There are inside jokes, and I just kind of . . . blank out for a bit. I guess this was a wash. I'll start making my own new memories tomorrow with Lucas. It'll be nice to hang out at some of the same downtown places as Melissa and Jessica.

"Um, hello, Peyton?" Madison says in an annoyed voice.

I snap back to attention. "Yes?"

"Oh, am I interrupting something?" Madison says with a laugh, while the other girls shift uncomfortably.

"Sorry, I was just thinking about this box I found buried in my backyard."

"What was in the box?" Skylar asks at the same time Madison pretends to gag.

"It has all these items from 1989—"

"So like you're totally going through someone's buried junk?" Madison sticks her tongue out. "So gross."

I open my mouth to respond, but realize that I don't think there's anything I can say to change Madison's mind. The rest of the girls seem cool, at least.

Then again, Madison does have a point. Rummaging through someone's buried junk is a little weird and might end up being a total waste of time. But there's something in my gut that tells me I'm onto something.

"What should we do?" Madison lies down on the couch. "I'm so bored."

"What do you guys usually do?" I ask.

"We watch videos, play around with makeup, dress up, hang by the pool, you know," Madison explains.

"Oh, you totally have to come over for Madison's pool party next week," Izzy says to me. "You could meet so many people."

"That would be great, thanks!" I look at Madison, who technically should be the one to invite me, but she isn't saying anything.

I'm wondering how I can leave here with Izzy's, Patrice's, and Skylar's info and if there's a way just the four of us could hang out. But then I would be leaving Madison out—kind of like she's doing to me.

"So bored," Madison sings.

An idea hits me. I reach into my backpack. "Hey, do you guys want to make friendship bracelets?" I pull out the strings I got to make Lily a bracelet like the one in the box.

"Oh, yes! Fashion!" Madison replies, sitting down cross-legged on the carpeted floor. Everybody gathers around in a circle as I start handing out colors and demonstrating how to start the braid.

It's quiet as we all begin to work.

"Who else have you met, Peyton?" Izzy asks.

"Oh, not a lot of people," I reply as I tighten up my braid. "Lucas Ryan."

The room goes still.

"Oh, do you guys know Lucas—"

"Of course, we know Lucas," Madison says, shifting uncomfortably.

"Yeah, he's been helping me with the box. He's super smart—"

"Should we order pizza?" Madison cuts me off.

The rest of the girls look down at the floor.

"I'm sorry," I say even though this time I don't know what I'm apologizing for. "Is there something I should know?"

"What's there to know?" Madison snaps at me. "Look, it's like beyond tragic what happened with Lucas, okay? But it's not like we were friends with him or anything before, so like why should I be expected to include him in things now, you know?"

Ah, no, I don't know. AT ALL what is going on.

Madison groans. "My mom keeps going on and on that I should invite him to my pool party, but it's like, um, Mom, why, when all he can do is sit around and not even get in the pool?" Madison's cheeks are flushed. "Plus, I know I'm supposed to be nice to him and all because of the accident, but he's a nerd, okay. It has nothing to do with him using a wheelchair."

A simmering starts in my stomach. Lucas was the first person to welcome me in this town.

"He's nice," Skylar speaks up.

"You're just saying that because you feel sorry for him," Madison replies.

"No, I'm not." Skylar dips her head down.

I've never been the kind of person who could stand up to a bully. Lily used to do it all the time. If anybody made a mean comment about girls playing soccer or made fun of anybody on the team, she'd confront the person and wouldn't back down. One time a mom of an opposing team member told Lily to "go back to where she came from" after Lily scored a goal. Lily marched right up to her and explained that she was born in the United States and then had the referee kick the mom out of the game for her racist comment.

I was so proud of Lily then. I wish I could be like her, but . . . could I really blow up the opportunity to make new friends, for Lucas?

Lucas, who immediately got excited about the box and offered to help me.

Lucas, who has introduced me to his family, and Frannie's ice cream, and is giving me a tour of his favorite places tomorrow.

Lucas, who is really funny and smart and is starting to pick up on some of my quirks.

Lucas, who's a kind person.

Madison sighs as she flips her shiny hair. "I just don't want to deal with it."

And that does it.

I get up to leave. "And I suddenly don't want to deal with you."

Patrice tells her to apologize, but it doesn't matter. I've seen Madison for who she really is. Patrice, Skylar, and Izzy are cool, but if they come with Madison, it's a hard pass.

"Are you seriously leaving because of Lucas Ryan?" Madison scoffs at me.

"Hey, thanks so much for having me over," I say with my voice dripping with fake sweetness. "You've proved that there are some things small and big towns have in common. Mean girls."

With that I storm out of the house and text my father to come get me immediately.

And I have no regrets.

CHAPTER TWELVE

1989

"Puking! Yes!" Jess practically screams before she takes a large sip of her strawberry milkshake at Wilz's soda fountain.

"Oh my goodness, Jess!" I cover my eyes in embarrassment. I can't even imagine what everybody must be thinking of us. I slowly remove my hands to see a few disgusted looks from the other customers.

"But seriously," Jess says in a quieter voice, so like a normal speaking voice for most. "Your mom's been sick every morning for a week. She has to be pregnant."

"I think so, too." I almost don't want to say it. Don't want to have that hope out there in case it isn't true.

Dad is usually gone by seven, so he hasn't seen it, but I've noticed the time Mom spends in the bathroom. How pale she looks. Same thing happened this morning.

It's taking everything I have to not ask her. And I am not one to show restraint!

"Okay, you need to be extra nice to your mom," Jess tells me. "And don't let her work too hard. My dad hired a housekeeper when my mom was pregnant because he didn't want her on her feet a lot."

I play with my straw. Jess knows we can't afford a housekeeper. But I can be better about cleaning my room, and I'll start dusting the piano and cleaning up after myself more. Maybe I'll even make my mom breakfast one morning.

She'll probably assume I want something.

"When do you think she's going to tell me?" I ask.

Jess looks thoughtful. "I don't know. Probably soon. And you'll have to run straight to the phone to tell me. Well, after giving your mom the biggest hug in the world."

Soon. My life is going to change so much in just a little while. I'm excited by the idea of a baby, but another part of me kind of wants to hold on to everything now, just as it is.

"I'm going to have a big family," Jess states with a confident nod.

"How many kids do you want?" I take a large sip of my chocolate milkshake.

She tilts her head to the side. One of the many, many things I love about Jess is that she always takes time to really think about the questions I ask her. "Well, I think about Jordan having five siblings, and that sounds great. To have all those people to rely on."

"And be in a band!" I add, since Jordan's older brother, Jonathan, is also in New Kids.

"So true!" Jess stares at her plastic straw. Her mouth turns down.

"What's wrong?"

"I wish I had a brother or sister," she says quietly. "I know I got worried about my parents not loving me as much if my mom gave birth, but it would just be nice to have a bigger family."

We're both only children, but it never bothered me as much as her.

"But we have each other," I remind her.

"Of course!" She reaches out, and we hold hands for a moment.

"No matter if it's a girl or a boy, my first child will be called Mel!"

I love her so much. That's such a wonderful idea.

"And I'm going to name my first child Jessica or Jesse!" I tell her. I never thought about it before, but I obviously have to.

"Our names work so well for either a boy or girl!"

"We have *the best* names!"

"The best!" Jess yells out. "And I'm going to be a doctor."

Jess is smart enough. She loves science and math. And she's also really good at taking care of people. Last summer, I wiped out on my bike. My knee was bloody, and it stung. Jess biked to her house in record time and came back with a first aid kit. She patched me up *and* even gave me a lollipop after. She'll make the best doctor.

Not me. I'm more into music and art. "I'm going to be a fashion designer. Or a model! Or singer!"

"You can be all three," she suggests.

It's exciting to think about the future. Where we'll be in ten, twenty, even thirty years. Oh my goodness, we'll be in our forties. We'll be so old!

"I know what we should do this afternoon!" Jess says. "To get you ready for your job as a model, singer, fashion designer, let's go to your house, get dressed up, and you can play another concert for me. But this time we'll do all fun songs."

"YES!" I scream, not caring about everybody else at the counter.

"And you have to play 'Lost in Your Eyes' first. It sounds exactly like the record."

"Oh! What if . . . ," I start off and am already shaking with excitement. "What if I start writing my own songs just like Debbie Gibson? I could maybe open up for New Kids one day!"

"Just like they did for Tiffany!"

"And then I'd become even more famous than them!"

"You'd be a cover girl! *Oh, oh-oh, you're a cover giiiirl!*" Jess sings along to another of our favorite New Kids songs. "Well, we better start right away!"

Before we leave, Jess grabs the coaster under her milk-shake. "For the time capsule, even though this soda fountain will be here for forever."

We take our bikes and ride the ten minutes to my house, singing our favorite songs on the way.

Jess jumps the steps to our front porch before taking a few rocks back and forth on our porch swing. It's something she always does. It makes me smile whenever I curl up on the swing to read.

"Are you ready to rock, Lake Springs?" I say as I open up the front door.

But as soon as we get inside, something is off.

Dad is home.

He's sitting on the couch, his hands and clothes dirty with grease from the cars he works on. Mom is sitting beside him and looks worried.

"Hi, Mr. Davis," Jess hesitantly greets him. She doesn't see him as much as my mom.

Dad looks up. He has a scowl on his face.

"Girls, go to Melissa's room," Mom says softly.

"Oh, I was going to play the piano for Jess—"

"Melissa," Mom says firmly. "Go to your room."

I don't understand why she's mad at me. I haven't done anything wrong.

"No, she should stay," Dad says in a gruff voice. "She's old enough to know."

Know what? Jess squeezes my hand. Wait, does this mean they're going to tell me that I'm going to have a baby brother or sister?

Mom gives me a nervous smile. "Yes, of course, she's old enough." Her attention turns toward Jess. "But listen, Jessica, honey, I think that maybe you should go home. Melissa can call you later."

"Oh, okay." Jess gives me a big hug. "Talk to you later."

"Yeah." I feel a lump form in my throat. I'm so nervous. I've never had one of those conversations where everything can change. This is a big moment.

I'm going to be a big sister!

"Sit down," Mom instructs me. I go to sit opposite my parents. When I walk by Dad, I smell the cigarette smoke that lingers on him after a night out with his friends. He's looking down at the floor. I can see the top of his balding head. He usually wears a baseball hat to cover it up.

"What's going on?" I ask, pretending that I don't know that I'm going to get some most excellent news.

"Everything is fine," Mom replies.

"No, it isn't, Janine," Dad grumbles.

Mom keeps her voice even. "Your father lost his job."

"Those guys fired me." But he didn't say "guys." If I repeated what word he used, Mom would stick a bar of soap in my mouth.

"What?" This isn't the news I was expecting. "What does that mean?"

"What it means," Dad says with a snarl, "is that you are no longer wasting money on stupid magazines and lunches with your little friend."

"But it's my money," I protest. I earn it through chores, and I can spend it how I like.

"Where do you think that money comes from? Do you think it grows on trees?"

I stay silent since anything I say will get me in trouble.

"No, of course you don't." Dad gets up from the couch. Mom reaches out her hand, but he yanks his away. He sees a *Teen Beat* magazine on the counter. "You need to start learning the value of money. This!" He picks up the magazine. "Is junk."

And then my father tears the magazine in two. And again. I watch as torn pictures of Joey, Jordan, Donnie, Danny, and Jonathan float down to the carpet.

I can feel the tears burn behind my eyes.

"Frank, please don't," Mom pleads. She seems nervous. "This isn't Melissa's fault."

"Oh, and it's mine?"

"That's not—" Mom takes a deep breath. "I'll pick up some shifts at the diner."

"Are you saying I can't provide for my family?"

"You know I'm not, and you need—"

"Do NOT tell me what to do," Dad snaps and raises his hand. Mom recoils.

Tears are now running down my face. I've never seen him this angry. And I don't know what this all means.

"Melissa, go to your room," Mom says in a calm voice.

I don't hesitate. I run into my room and slam the door shut.

Voices start drifting up. I throw a pillow over my head, but I can still hear the yelling. It's never been this bad before.

I remove the pillow and put on my headphones. I rewind my *Hangin' Tough* tape on my Walkman until I get to "Please Don't Go Girl" and put the volume on high, even though I'm not supposed to move the dial above four to protect my hearing.

I curl up on my side as Joey starts singing. I stare into one of the posters on my walls and concentrate on his blue eyes. Problem is, I *do* want to go away right now. I want to be any-where but here.

I jump when there's a knock on my door. I'm sure I'm going to get in trouble for something. I always have to be less *me* when Dad's home.

"Honey," Mom says as she opens the door. She sits down and looks tired. "It's going to be okay. Your father is upset, which is understandable. Just give him some time to cool down." She glances at the door and drops her voice. "And maybe you should hang out at Jess's this week. I can call her parents to make sure it's okay. In fact, I'll ask them if you can spend the night. Wouldn't that be fun?"

I nod because that's about the only thing I want to do right now. I want to get out of this house and away from my dad.

"Are you okay?" she asks as she brushes back my hair.

"Yes," I say, even though I'm not okay. I'm confused. I sniff as Mom wipes away the tears on my face. "I thought you were going to tell me you were pregnant."

"What?" Mom's eyes go wide before looking at the door. "How do you know?" she asks in a low whisper.

"Morning sickness." Wait, this means . . . "So you are? That's so great!"

Mom gets up and closes my bedroom door. "Melissa, honey, your father doesn't know. And I can't tell him right now because he's under too much stress."

"But you're going to start showing."

She frowns, and her entire forehead is creased with worry. "Not for another month or so. Listen, I need this to be a secret just between the two of us for a little while, okay? This isn't the time to spring this on your father."

"Okay." I want to celebrate the fact that I'm going to be a big sister. I'm going to be the best big sister in the whole wide world. But I also don't want to make Dad any more upset.

"Melissa, I'm serious. You can't tell anybody."

"I know."

Mom tilts her head at me. "That also means Jessica."

"But, Mom!"

"No *buts*. I mean it. Just for a few weeks, until I can figure everything out. Nobody can know. Nobody."

I don't reply. How could I not tell Jess?

I could never keep a secret from my best friend.

CHAPTER THIRTEEN

"Welcome to bustling downtown Lake Springs!" Lucas announces as he gestures toward the three blocks of Main Street.

Perhaps *bustling* might not be the correct term. In fact, it's the complete opposite of what's going on in front of us.

There are no other people currently on the sidewalks of downtown. This block has four storefronts that are empty. There are only seven cars parked on the street.

I'm sure at one point Lake Springs was, in fact, bustling. There had to be a reason people settled here, and it couldn't solely be the college.

Lucas looks at the receipt in his hand and moves toward one of the empty storefronts. "This is it: 128 Main Street."

We both look at the narrow store, with a For Sale sign in the window. We peer inside and see a few bare shelves lining the wall.

"So this was Book World." I press my nose against the window, hoping to see something to prove that it was a bookstore once upon the eighties.

While we wait for the film to develop—which can take five to seven business days, we learned—we decided to go downtown to visit the places on the coaster and two receipts.

"Well, this answers absolutely nothing," I reply.

"Now, hold on, hold on. This is where Melissa and Jessica bought"—Lucas looks down at the receipt—"four items that totaled nine dollars and forty-five cents. At least we know they weren't psychopaths, since they liked to read. Although . . . I'm wondering if they bought magazines, given the cost. My mom said that entire wall on the right was filled with different types of magazines. Hundreds."

I didn't even realize there were that many magazines out there. My dad gets one that has a bunch of long articles. There are a couple of cartoons, but only with one illustration and then some line I never understand. I thought cartoons are supposed to be funny, but not these. Dad says I'll appreciate the humor when I'm older. We'll see.

"What's going on?" Lucas says. "You don't seem that excited."

Of course I'm not that excited.

All I get from the box are a whole lot of dead ends. Plus, my "playdate" was one big disaster. And Lily and I could only talk for ten minutes last night because she was meeting up with our—well, my *former*—soccer team. So, basically, my initial suspicions were right: Worst. Summer. Ever.

"I mean, it's an empty bookstore. How is this going to help with figuring out what happened? Or anything at all?" I've never been the kind of person to give up, but there's a first time for everything.

"Ah, I thought that it would be a good way for me to show you downtown—through Melissa and Jessica's footsteps. Two birds, one stone, you know?"

"Don't I!" I reply quietly and then hang my head because Lily isn't here to think it's funny.

"Has anybody ever told you that you can be quite odd?" Lucas says with a snort.

"Oh, *I'm* odd?"

He sits up a bit straighter. "I prefer the term *unique*."

"I mean, that's one word for it," I fire back.

Lucas furrows his brows. "Okay, what's this all about?"

"What's what all about?"

He grimaces. "Your mood. Is it about the box, because we've only just started on our quest . . . or is this about the other L in your life?"

"Her name is Lily."

Lucas gives me a kind smile. "When you talk about things you used to do back home, your voice is all excited, especially when you go all jock on me about soccer. But there's also this sadness. I know I'm a boy and all, but we are capable of having a range of emotions, including feeling down when you're missing someone." Lucas's cheeks get a little ruddy. "You know, in case you ever want to talk about it."

I'm speechless for a moment. Usually, the only person who could figure out things about me by paying attention to what I'm *not* saying is . . . Lily. I appreciate the gesture and all, but one thing I like about the box is how it helps distract me from missing her.

He clears his throat. "But I can also be incredibly—and I do mean *incredibly*—macho if you want to talk about anything else."

This *macho* dude needs to get out of my head.

"It's just I'm getting the feeling that maybe this is all hopeless," I finally admit. I'm not just talking about the box. Living in Lake Springs. Trying to fit in here. "It was silly for me to think that I could figure out something that happened thirty years ago from a few pieces of junk in a box."

"No!" Lucas cries out. "Why would you say that? We've only just started. Yeah, it's not like visiting a few stores is going to do anything, but we're still waiting on the photos and have that code to crack. Come on, this is fun. I mean, you get to hang out with me, which is a prize unto itself, if I do say so myself. Which I just did."

I can't help but crack the tiniest of smiles.

"Ah, see! You know that I'm right! Besides, do you have anything better to do?" He raises his eyebrow at me.

He has a point.

"Okay, let's get to it. Downtown." Lucas pushes up his glasses, a look of concentration on his face. He gestures out to Main Street. "This is a place where Melissa and Jessica must've spent a lot of time. Just imagine it. Thirty years in the past."

I step away from the storefront and try to picture this place filled with books. An excitement starts swirling in my belly knowing that Melissa and Jessica were here at some point. Two girls who lived in this town over three decades ago. In a way, they're like a fantasy. But I do want to know more about them to make them feel real.

And Lucas is right. This glimpse into their life, as small as it is, makes me feel like I'm moving forward.

To where, I don't know. But it's better than being stuck.

Not that I'm going to tell him he's right.

"It's sad that it's gone," I say.

Lucas nods. "Yeah, my grandparents always talk about how much downtown changed since SuperMart opened nearby."

Looking at the empty storefronts, I can see their point.

"Listen, I know we've hit some stumbles, but I love nothing more than a good mystery. I'm all about figuring out what everything means, especially that coded letter. Plus, I'm nosy, although I prefer the term *inquisitive*." Lucas narrows his eyes as he studies me. "Which leads me to this: Why do *you* want to figure out what happened? Because, yeah, mystery and all that, but I don't know. I feel like it's something more."

Again, how does he know this stuff about me?

I don't hesitate. "I want to understand how two best friends could end their friendship."

Lucas gives me a look. I'm pretty sure he can tell I'm not just talking about Melissa and Jessica. "Well, we don't know for sure that's what happened."

"There's an apology note that says, 'Please forgive me.' Half of a necklace was buried. That doesn't feel like something two besties would bury together."

I know in my gut that something bad happened between them. It could also be because without this box, I never would have met Lucas and I have no idea what I'd be doing right now.

So maybe I found the box because I needed to.

"Okay, you have a point," Lucas admits. "Plus, do you know what this is? Freedom!" Lucas spins his wheelchair around in a circle. "I still can't believe my mom let me go downtown by myself. I mean, not like it was easy."

At our dinner at Lucas's house, he mentioned he wanted to give me a tour. Ms. Ryan had lots of suggestions for where we could go, but Lucas didn't want her hovering. So his sister, Zoe, said she was meeting friends at the coffee shop right off Main Street today. She offered to take us and said she would only be a couple of blocks away. For a moment, I didn't think

Ms. Ryan was going to cave, but then both my parents said they thought it was a wonderful idea, and that sort of pushed her to agree.

So that's how Lucas and I were let out into the wilds of downtown Lake Springs.

"You don't understand; she hardly leaves me out of her sight." Lucas takes two fingers and points them at his eyes and then at me. "She's on constant watch."

"What about your other friends? Does she let you go out with them?"

Lucas snorts.

"I mean, she has to let you hang out with friends," I reason. I'm not allowed to go to places by myself, but my parents have never minded dropping me off somewhere if they knew Lily or another soccer friend would be there.

"Yeah. I guess . . ." Lucas looks across the street where two kids on skateboards fly by. "I'm not a total loner. My buddies Connor and Alec are both away right now. Connor is at coding camp, and Alec is on vacation. I make a lot of other people uncomfortable now," Lucas states as he begins to wheel down the block.

My mind flashes back to yesterday when the room got quiet at the mention of Lucas's name.

This is the only version of Lucas that I know. I can't picture him any other way.

Maybe we both came into each other's lives for a reason.

"Well," he says with a little too much effort. "The good news is that Wilz's is still around."

We pass by a few more stores—an antique shop, a women's clothing store, and a sushi restaurant.

"How's the sushi?" I had sushi for the first time a few months ago. Lily's parents took us, and we felt very fancy and grown-up, even though neither of us dared to try the raw fish. Yuck.

Lucas shrugs as he points to six stairs that lead to the front door. "Haven't had the pleasure."

"Oh." Then I think of something. I did a couple of internet searches after realizing Lucas uses a wheelchair. "Isn't there some kind of law about public places having to be accessible?"

"Please don't tell me you did research on having a friend who uses a wheelchair." Lucas shakes his head.

"No!" I mean, not really, but I did want to have a better understanding of what life is like for him.

Lucas gives me a look that shows that he doesn't believe me. Fair enough.

"So, yes, there's the Americans with Disabilities Act, which does state that public places should be accessible; however, older buildings—and that's exactly all you'll find downtown—can get away with being inaccessible if it costs too much to make changes."

I look at the six steps. Not a big deal for most people, but a huge obstacle for Lucas.

"That's not fair," I say.

"It's okay. I've heard their sushi is gross, and I can do without a side of food poisoning, thank you very much." Lucas moves on without another glance. "Besides, there's somewhere even better that we're going to for lunch, *and* it has to do with the box. But first . . ."

Lucas stops in the front of Wilz's Drug Store. It has a long window filled with a few Minnesota Vikings hats and T-shirts, as well as signs about prescriptions.

A bell rings as we enter. Soft music is playing overhead. There are some clothes at the front of the store and then aisles and aisles of products: shampoos, soaps, medicines, and so on.

I glance at the round blue-and-red coaster in my hand with the Wilz's logo, color faded. "Why would there be a coaster from a drugstore?"

Lucas gestures to the far corner where there's a long counter with stools. It's an old-fashioned soda fountain . . . that's empty.

"They used to serve ice cream and sundaes here, so that's probably where it was from."

I have to be honest: Lake Springs was a lot cooler in the 1980s. Everything now is either abandoned or quiet.

"Hello, Lucas." An older woman approaches us. "Do you need anything?"

"No worries, Mrs. McGraw, I don't plan on knocking over any displays today. I wanted to show my friend the soda counter."

"Ah yes." A sad smile settles on her lips. "It's a shame. They made the most delicious egg creams back when I was your age."

This gives me an idea. "So you've lived here all your life?"

"Why, yes I have!"

I produce the photo of Melissa and Jessica. "Would you happen to know who either of these two girls were, or are? This photo was taken in 1989."

Mrs. McGraw puts on the glasses that were hanging from her neck and studies the faces. "I'm sorry, dear, I don't have the slightest clue. There were a lot of kids that came and went in this town."

I take the photo back, feeling defeated yet again. "Thanks anyways."

What if Melissa and Jessica didn't live in Lake Springs at all? What if they came here to visit someone and then buried the box?

I study the two receipts. The Book World one was from June 17, 1989, and the Kitchen Corner was from June 30, 1989. It could've been a summer vacation.

Lucas snaps me back to the present. "Hey, Peyton, I'm going to need some help here."

"Yeah, what's up?" I ask as I see him glancing back at me.

"They put in a new display that's blocking my usual route to turn around so we can leave."

I look at the shelves only a foot away from us. The entire display is filled with candles. Glass candles.

"I knocked over a card display once, and it was a whole ordeal, and well, this would be a lot louder and more expensive."

"Sure, what can I do?"

Lucas puts his hands in his lap. "I need you to drive."

I go behind Lucas and grab the two handles on the back of the chair. I reverse slowly, noting the infamous card display behind me. I try to turn him to avoid the front table with the Fourth of July display, but it's tight.

I think about when my parents try to parallel park their car and sometimes have to inch forward and then backward to slowly turn into a space. So I try that tactic. Little by little, I'm able to maneuver Lucas around.

An older couple walks into the drugstore and stops and stares.

"She only has a learner's permit," Lucas remarks sarcastically.

"I'm almost there."

I bite my lip as I concentrate on the final turns. I can see why Lucas didn't want to do it; it would be so easy to misjudge and cause the entire display to crash.

Or he could just want me to take the blame if I knock anything over.

Honestly, it's a toss-up.

After a couple of more turns, we clear the obstacles and reach the safety of outside.

"Now to the good part." Lucas picks up speed as we cross the street to Mimi's Café. "This used to be the Kitchen Corner, so I figured we could have lunch here in honor of Melissa and Jessica."

"Sounds great." My stomach growls. I haven't eaten out since we got here. Save dinner at Lucas's, it's been cereal for breakfast, sandwiches for lunch, and whatever Dad feels like pulling together for dinner, which has been either chicken nuggets or frozen pizza. Mom loves to cook. She used to make a huge brunch spread on the weekends, but she hasn't been around.

I open the door for Lucas. There are already a few tables full of diners. This is the most people I've seen in this city so far. Except for one teenager with brown skin, the rest are all white.

A woman with stark white hair with a purple-and-white bow greets us warmly. "Well hello, Lucas. Who's your friend?" She pulls away a chair at the first table near the window, and Lucas moves into its place as I sit across from him.

"This is Peyton. She's new to town, so I had to introduce her to Lake Springs' finest burger of cheese."

"Why thank you!" The woman looks outside. "Is your mom parking?"

"If you can believe it, Mimi, Mom is letting me dine by myself."

"Good for you." She gives him a wink.

"I did tell her that you'd cut up my food into tiny pieces and give me a sippy cup."

She playfully swats Lucas's arm. "You are too much, Lucas. Your mama is just doing her best. So! Two cheeseburgers and fries?"

"Yes, please," I reply, thinking about Melissa and Jessica's order. They also got Cherry Cokes, but I don't really drink soda. My parents never let me as a kid, and when I finally had a Coke I didn't like it.

"I know Lucas wants the finest natural water the many lakes of Minnesota can provide. What can I get you to drink, hon?"

"I'm good with water, too, thanks."

"Got it!" Mimi heads to behind the counter.

"Hey, I forgot to ask you how yesterday at Madison's went," Lucas says.

Ugh. Just another thing I want to forget.

"You were right," I admit.

"A sentiment you should become familiar with," he replies with a smug grin.

"I mean, I thought Izzy, Patrice, and Skylar were cool and all, but Madison is just a basic mean girl. And they seem like a package deal."

I don't tell Lucas what Madison said about him. He doesn't need to hear it, although I think he's probably more than aware of what kids say behind his back.

"Yeah, Madison likes to collect things, including friends, but I knew you were smart enough to see through her."

"Wait a second, are you giving me a compliment?" I tease him. It's pretty clear Lucas is the brains of this operation.

Lucas ignores me and reaches into the side pocket of his wheelchair to pull out a piece of paper. "Okay, let's get down to business! I've made a list."

"Of what?"

He gestures toward outside. "Since downtown can be a bit boring, I felt I needed to come up with other places to show you in Lake Springs. Because as I have learned, you have to make the best with the hand you've been dealt, and that includes where you live."

He has a point. This is my home now, so I better get used to that fact.

"Okay, closer to the middle school is one of my favorite places: the skate park. I enjoy nothing more than watching overconfident dudes fall on their faces." Lucas lets out a loud laugh that sounds like a horn; a few people turn to look at him, but he doesn't seem to notice. "Okay, the library is awesome as you know because, library. On Monday afternoons they have a teen movie, but we'd still be able to go as long as your parents say it's okay if it's PG-13. So they show some movie, sometimes it's newer, oftentimes it'll be a few decades old—oh! We can request movies, so maybe we should do *Batman* from 1989 since Melissa and Jessica went. But anyway, my favorite part about movie days is that one of the volunteers always brings these amazing baked goods. I dream about her lemon bars. And she always has nut-free options, so you'll be good to stuff your face."

That does sound fun *and* delicious.

"Okay!" Lucas pushes up his glasses. "Next up on Lucas's List of Lake Springs Not Being All That Bad is Prairie View Park. In the summer they have Family Fun Night on Tuesdays. They have some band come and play in the gazebo, and the VFW hall does a cookout. On Thursdays they host movie nights. We usually go unless it's been rainy, as this thing does not like mud. I once got stuck, and if you think that incredibly slow turn you did back at Wilz's was embarrassing—"

"I wasn't embarrassed," I state.

Lucas shakes his head. "With how long it took you, you should be."

"Hey!" I was just trying to help!

Mimi comes over and places two red baskets in front of Lucas and me. The smell instantly makes my mouth water.

"Luckily the next few days are supposed to be sunny, so we should totally go to the concert. I'm fairly certain my mom will insist you come. If you already couldn't tell from the fuss she made the other night, she gets excited about new people. And to let you in on a Ryan sibling secret, Zoe is having lunch with her boyfriend today, which Mom has no idea about because if you think she made a scene with you guys, it was nothing compared to the horror of Zoe's homecoming date last year. There were multiple cameras set up. That's *multiple*. We never heard from Chris again. Rumor has it he's working on an oil rig in Alaska."

Lucas picks up his cheeseburger and takes a huge bite. He sees me staring at him.

"I'm joking. Well, not about the cameras. She hired a *professional photographer*, Peyton. For a school dance."

At least his mom is involved. There has to be some kind of happy medium between his mom hovering and my mom being MIA.

I take a bite of the cheeseburger, and my eyes practically roll into the back of my head it's so good. Thick, juicy patty and melted cheddar on a soft white bun. Way better than the fast food we usually pick up on the way back from a game.

"Just wait until I take you to the popcorn stand. Best popcorn ever, trust me."

It's only been a few days, but I do trust Lucas. He was right about Frannie's ice cream; he was right about these burgers. He has yet to lead me astray.

"See," he says as he takes another big bite. "Living here isn't so bad."

I nod as I shove a perfectly crisp french fry into my mouth.

He may be right.

CHAPTER FOURTEEN

1989

"Remember what I told you," Mom says as we walk into Kitchen Corner a couple of hours later. "This is our secret."

"Well, look who it is!" Her friend Mimi comes from behind the counter to give us both a hug. Her brown hair is in a high bun.

"Hey, Mimi!" I give her a smile even though I don't feel like smiling.

"Please tell me you're willing to pick up some shifts next week," Mimi says to Mom as she shoves a pencil behind her ear. "We're going to get slammed with the parade for the Fourth."

Mom glances at me. "That might work."

Guess Jess isn't the only person I'm expected to keep secrets from. I don't even want to think how Dad would react if Mom started working behind his back.

"Hi!" Jess says as she walks in. "I'm so excited for you to

come over! My parents are going to pick us up in an hour. So dinner is on them!" Jess waves a ten-dollar bill.

"That's very thoughtful of your parents, but Melissa can pay for her own meal." Mom hands me five dollars. I take the money, but know I'm not going to spend it. Dad would get mad. Mom already told him that I was having dinner at the Millers' house, but since Jess's parents have some hospital board meeting, they recommended Jess and I meet here to eat, and they'll pick us up after. Kitchen Corner does have the best burgers.

"Okay, you be good," Mom says with a kiss on my cheek.

"Before you leave, Mrs. Davis, can you please take our picture?" Jess asks as she hands my mom her camera.

"Of course!"

Jess and I lean over our table and smile as Mom presses the button.

"I hope I did that okay. I take the worst pictures." Mom hands Jess the camera.

"Thank you so much!"

"You're welcome." Mom turns and shoots me a stern look. "Please remember our conversation."

"Yes" is all I can say before she gives me a goodbye hug. She holds me more firmly than normal, and I hug her back tightly.

Jess waits a few seconds after my mom leaves before

she leans in. "Did your mom tell you about the baby?" she whispers.

Nobody can know, Melissa, nobody, Mom's warning echoes in my ears.

But Mom didn't say I couldn't tell her about Dad.

"I have to tell you a secret," I start, even though I have no idea if it's even a secret. Won't people figure it out when my father is no longer working at the garage? "My dad lost his job."

Jess gasps. "Is that why he was home today? He looked angry."

He always looks angry, I want to tell her, but I don't.

Instead, I reply, "I don't think he wants people to know."

Jess nods along. "What does that mean?"

I don't know. "I guess he'll get another job."

That should be easy, right? That's what adults do. They get jobs and work. He's worked at Ben's Tires since I've been alive. He can probably get a job at one of the other places in town. I'm sure it'll be easy and he'll be back to work in no time.

Jess tilts her head. "Are you okay? You seem off."

Maybe because I'm keeping a huge secret from my best friend.

I don't feel like I can tell her anything. And I don't like it at all.

"Yeah. Just tired." I try to focus on the positive. "But it's good! I'm here with you! We're going to have cheeseburgers!"

I don't want to talk about my family anymore because it'll mean I have to lie. I can't do that to Jess.

"Yes, the *best* cheeseburgers," Jess confirms.

Mimi comes over with a smile. "Well, I can already guess what you two are going to have."

"Two cheeseburgers, two fries, and two Cherry Cokes, please!" we sing in unison. It's an order we do a lot.

"One, two, three, you owe me a *Cherry* Coke!" Jess says with a laugh, even though we both know she'll be the one paying for my drink. And cheeseburger. And fries.

"Oh!" Jess sits up. "We should put the receipt from here in our box!"

"Yes! That sounds perfect," I reply. Whoever finds it will have to know where they can get the most delicious cheeseburgers in the history of cheeseburgers.

I'm already feeling a little less sad being with Jess. She makes everything not only bearable, but better, too. So much better.

We see some high school guys walk past the window, one wearing a black T-shirt with a yellow Batman logo.

"Hey!" Jess exclaims. "That's the same shirt Jordan wore on *The Arsenio Hall Show*! We should go see the movie. It came out last weekend."

"It looks dark, and I don't like that Prince song." Even though it doesn't look that fun, movies also cost money. Two dollars for kids. I don't even know if I have an allowance anymore, but I probably have enough change in my piggy bank if Jess really wants to go.

Mom has her secrets, and I can have mine, too. Dad doesn't have to know everything.

"Yeah, that song is weird. There's hardly any singing—it's all talking from the movie." Jess scrunches up her nose. "But everybody is talking about it. Or we could see *Honey, I Shrunk the Kids*. Amy said it was hilarious."

Amy. We haven't really seen Amy or anybody else since the sleepover last weekend, but I guess she and Jess talk. Which is totally fine. Not a big deal.

She continues, "I'm excited to see a superhero on the big screen. My dad loved those Superman movies from a few years ago. I'm hoping this means there'll be a Wonder Woman movie soon."

"Oh yes!"

Wonder Woman is THE BEST. And if they're making a Batman movie, that must mean Wonder Woman will be next. She is the greatest superhero of all time, after all. Jess and I would sometimes twirl around in the backyard like Lynda Carter did in that TV show that's in reruns during the day.

Our cheeseburgers are placed in front of us, and I take a delicious bite.

Maybe this summer can turn around.

"We have some exciting news!" Mrs. Miller says when we arrive back to their house an hour later.

"What is it?" Jess replies.

"Come and sit down. The meeting with the hospital was very interesting."

"Oh!" Jess seems excited, while I'm confused how any kind of work meeting would be interesting.

My dad would never tell me about his day. Maybe I should start asking?

"The hospital system has taken on a smaller hospital in Springfield about an hour away," Dr. Miller begins to explain. "They need an ear, nose, and throat specialist, so I'm going to go there one day a week to see patients from that county."

"And if things go well, your father might be promoted to chief doctor at the hospital." Mrs. Miller beams at her husband.

So my father got fired, while Jess's dad got promoted.

I push down the jealousy that's starting to creep in. I shouldn't be jealous of all that Jess has. I *shouldn't*, but . . .

Jess's face falls for a moment. "So you're commuting one day a week, but might for five days?"

Jess's parents exchange a look. I don't know what it means, but usually it's not good.

Dr. Miller clears his throat. "Well, for *now* it's one day a week, but if I get the promotion, we'll most likely move, but that's not—"

"This is an absolute disaster!" Jess shouts as she stands up and storms upstairs.

NO.

Jess can't be moving.

How did this summer take such an epic turn for the worse?

"Jessica!" her father calls after her. "Come back here right now!"

I feel sick to my stomach.

She doesn't deserve to have bad things happen to her.

Neither do I.

Or Mom.

Dr. Miller looks up at the staircase. "Honey, it's fine."

"No, it's not!" Jess screams from the top floor.

"Jessica Cynthia Miller, get down here this instant. You're being rude and dramatic."

Jess stomps down the stairs. I've never seen her like this. I want to stomp and scream, too. She can't move away. She just can't.

"How can I be calm when we're moving?" Jess then grabs me in a tight hug. I can feel her tears on my shoulder.

I start crying because Jess is crying.

This has now turned into the worst day ever.

"We are *not* moving," Dr. Miller replies firmly. "It's only one day a week to see how much need there is for a specialist. I'm simply helping out a smaller community. This is a good thing."

"You said we might move," Jess says through sobs.

"In years, sweetie. *Years.* And that's only if it's warranted. This would be a big decision and one we'll make *as a family.* I shouldn't have said anything."

"No, you shouldn't have," Mrs. Miller adds. "You've worked her up for no reason whatsoever."

"So you're not moving?" I ask for clarification. I'm already dealing with too much change. I can handle a new sibling and my dad losing his job, but I could never survive Jess moving away.

"We are not," Dr. Miller confirms.

"For now." Jess sticks her lower lip out.

"Jessica, we never know what the future will hold." Her mom reaches out to brush Jess's long hair. "But we're not moving anytime soon. Please smile, sweetheart."

Jess replies by grinding her teeth.

"I apologize to both you girls." Dr. Miller rubs a hand on his face. "I got carried away."

"You certainly did," Mrs. Miller says with a shake of her head. "Why don't you girls go upstairs and I'll bring up some ice cream?" She kisses Jess on the forehead.

"With whipped cream?" Jess asks through sniffles.

"With whipped cream *and* a cherry on top."

Okay, so maybe this isn't the worst day ever. As long as Jess isn't moving. Not like there's anything keeping my family here. Maybe Springfield will have a job for my dad? We could all move together! Because there is no way—and I mean *no way*—that I would ever let Jess move without me.

We hold hands as we go upstairs.

"I'm so sorry!" Jess hugs me again. "I got so upset and assumed the worst. Can you imagine if we moved?"

"I don't want to imagine that." Never. *Ever.*

We get to Jess's room, and she collapses on the fluffy pink rug on her floor. "What a day! I can't handle all of the drama. I know what we need." She gets up and hands me Teddy. Her parents gave her the small honey-colored teddy bear when they picked her up at the airport when she landed from South Korea as an infant. Teddy has a bow tie made out of the South Korean flag. Jess gives Teddy to me when I've had a bad day. Teddy spent the night with me at the hospital when I had my tonsils taken out (by her dad!) in second grade.

I really need him now. More than she even knows.

Jess puts a cassette into her stereo, and a slow song fills her room.

"You're my hero," Jess says to me as she holds my hand.

The song is "Wind Beneath My Wings" from the movie *Beaches*. It's about two girls who meet when they're younger and become the best of friends. It's sad since one of them dies as an adult, but I like to think Jess and I will be there for each other when we're older.

No matter what.

"Hey, Mel," Jess says as she gives my hand a squeeze. "I

know it might be scary about your dad and his job, but it's going to be okay. This is still going to be the best summer ever!"

I remain quiet. I want to believe her, but now I'm not so sure.

CHAPTER FIFTEEN

My parents always talk about the fact that "kids these days" don't have any patience. That we're used to instant gratification with our phones and the internet and social media.

They may have a point.

Not like I'd ever admit that to them. No way.

"Finally!" Lucas waves around an envelope when I walk into his house.

"Did you look at them?" I ask as I sit down at a chair in the dining room.

Lucas scoffs. "Do you think I'd do that to you? I figure you would've waited for me."

To be honest, I'm not too sure about that. No way could I show restraint when there might be some answers in the palm of my hand.

Lucas opens the envelope and starts laying out the pictures on the dining table.

The first is of the white girl, in the same outfit she was wearing in the photo that was in the box.

The second is of the white girl sticking her tongue out; the picture is slightly blurry.

The next is both of them standing on swings. It's not a great picture—the Asian girl's eyes are closed.

People really *didn't* have any idea if the pictures they took were any good.

"Hey! I know that place." Lucas taps his finger on the photo. "It's Prairie View Park. Wow, they really need to update their equipment. Those look like the same swings."

The next photo is of the Asian girl holding up a sign that says, "Love you, Mel."

"So that must be Jessica," I state. Now we're getting somewhere.

"Oh, wow. *WOW.*" He places down a few photos in a row of Melissa and Jessica posing with some of the pictures from the collage that was in the box. "Girls are so weird."

In one, the girl who must be Melissa is kissing a photo; in another, Jessica is on a pillow, gazing at a poster of a guy wearing a checkered vest and very poufy black hair.

"Yes, and boys are *totally* normal," I fire back.

"At least we agree on that," Lucas says while I groan. "Who are these guys? And clearly Melissa and Jessica need better taste."

For once, I finally have an answer.

After listening to their mix, I looked up a few of the artists. The singer of the second song, "I'll Be Loving You (Forever)" was not, in fact, a girl, but a guy with a high voice: Jordan Knight from New Kids on the Block. From the photos in front of us, it's clear that Jessica was a fan of Jordan, and Melissa liked Joey, who was the youngest member of the group.

"These guys are from a band that was popular back then: New Kids on the Block."

"So they're like the 1989 American version of BTS?"

I shrug. "I guess. They're still around and touring."

"What?" Lucas looks shocked. "How old are they now?"

"Must be in their fifties."

"They must be exhausted," Lucas remarks with a snort. "You know."

"Yeah, I'm sure." My parents are always talking about how tired they are, and they're not singing and dancing onstage.

"*You know* . . . ," Lucas says again while wiggling his eyebrows.

"So what's the next photo because—"

"*You know* . . ."

"Ah, I *don't know* because you aren't showing me the photos!" Why is he being so weird, well more than normal? Especially since we might get some answers; it's like he's purposely—

Wait. I get what he's doing. I *do* know.

"DON'T I!"

"There she is." He gives me a satisfied nod. "See, things haven't changed that much for you. *This* L in your life can handle your little, ah, eccentricities."

For a moment, I don't know what to say. I've never told Lucas about my inside joke with Lily, but I guess he's seen me randomly scream out "DON'T I" enough to figure it out. Figure *me* out.

"Thanks," I reply softly. It's such a small gesture, but it's a nice one. It's a way for me to hold on to something—as silly as it may be—from my past. "So what's next?"

Lucas's attention goes back to the photos in his hand; his eyes get wide. "Oh! We already know this place."

The photo is of the two of them at a restaurant. Its chairs and tables are different, but it's definitely Mimi's Café.

"So this might be from the receipt that's in the box," I say.

Huh. I wonder if I should've shown the photo to Mimi. What's the chance she'd remember two girls with all the people who come and go in a restaurant? That's even if she worked there when it was Kitchen Corner.

"What do you think that is?" I point to a pale circle in the corner.

"Oh, I guess whoever took the picture had their thumb in the way. It happens."

With each photo, it feels like the puzzle that is the box is slowly coming together, piece by piece. Even though we still have no idea what happened to Melissa and Jessica, at least we can get a better sense of who they were.

When Lucas puts down the next photo, I let out a gasp.

"What is it?" he asks.

It's of the two girls rocking on a chair swing on a front porch.

But it's not any front porch.

"That's my house."

Lucas is silent for a moment. "I mean, you did dig the box up in your backyard, so it would be easy to presume that one of them had lived in your house."

True, but still. Seeing them both in a place that I would sit and curl up reading makes this all the more real.

"What else do we have?"

He places down a few more pictures that all go together. They're of some kind of parade. People are dressed up in red, white, and blue. There's a guy in stilts who I assume is supposed to be Uncle Sam. A woman in green doing her best Lady Liberty.

"Does Lake Springs have a Fourth of July parade?" I ask, curious as it's only two days away. I haven't seen any signs about a parade or anything, really. We're going to Mom's new campus where they're having fireworks.

"Not anymore, or at least since I can remember."

"It looks like fun," I comment. There's a photo of the two girls, each holding snow cones in patriotic colors. Melissa's smile seems forced, though. Her brown eyes look sad.

It's the first time one of them doesn't look happy.

There's another one of two adults: a guy at a grill, holding up a hamburger patty. He's got a bald head and is wearing these bright checkered shorts. I'd be horrified if my dad ever wore anything that loud. Behind him is a woman with long strawberry blond hair pulled back on the sides.

"Maybe they're Melissa's parents?" I say, since they're white.

But Lucas doesn't reply. He's staring at the next photo.

"Peyton, I think you might be right."

"Well, that's not something I ever expected *you* to say. I mean, don't be shocked. There's a first time for—"

But I stop talking the second he sets down the picture.

It's always satisfying when I'm proven right, but this isn't a good feeling.

The last photo is of Jessica, a tear streaming down her face. She's holding up a sign that reads, "I'm sorry. I love you. You're still my best friend."

Something did go wrong.

Now we just need to figure out what.

After dinner, I pace my room.

How did they go from smiling faces to Melissa looking unhappy and Jessica in tears?

What happened on the Fourth of July?

This all is starting to feel familiar. No longer smiling and laughing. A rift between two best friends.

I call Lily, hoping she's somewhere she can talk. I'm worried about what's happening to us. Are we the new Melissa and Jessica?

"Peyton!" she answers. From the blue-painted wall behind her, I can tell she's in the living room. "Wow, are you actually around for once?"

"Um, you've been busy, too," I reply, because she has. Did she expect me to simply sit around and wait until she had time for me?

"I'm surprised you're not running around with Lucas. How's the crime fighting going, by the way?" She lets out a forced laugh that I don't like at all.

"We're not solving a crime," I state, my patience wearing thin. "Besides, you're always off with your friends."

"*Our* friends," she says with a frown. "It kills me that you're not here and all you're doing is sending me pictures about how you're moving on."

"What? Do you not want me to share my new life with you?"

"It's like you're rubbing it in." Lily purses her lips together.

"I didn't . . ." I'm not sure how to respond. I never thought that Lily would be the one jealous of me.

"But you did." She looks up and blinks really fast. It's something she does when she's fighting back tears. "It's really hard to be here surrounded by all of the places we'd hang out. And you've got all these new things and people in your life."

"That's not true," I reply. "I only really hang out with Lucas."

Lily scowls. "Ugh, yes, Lucas. Your new best friend."

"What about Callie?" It's something I've wanted to bring up since Lily first mentioned her. "All I hear from you when we do talk is about Callie."

"You're not here!" Lily practically screams.

"And you're not here!" I reply with the exact same tone. "So what? Are you saying that we were only friends because we lived near each other?"

"Maybe so," Lily says, and my heart shatters into a thousand pieces.

"I have to go," I say as I hang up.

I'm tired of Lily being the one who has to rush off because she has something better to do. I turn my phone off and throw it across the room.

Then I lay back in bed and let the tears come out.

Lily and I have never been in a fight before.

So, yeah, I guess I know exactly how Melissa and Jessica could drift apart.

CHAPTER SIXTEEN

1989

This might be the worst day yet.

The fighting started again early this morning. It's been quiet for nearly a half hour, so I tiptoe downstairs, hoping to avoid a confrontation.

I'm not so lucky.

"Just where do you think you're going?" Dad calls out from the couch.

He has dark bags under his eyes. He's in the same dirty T-shirt he wore yesterday. I'm not sure he's even left the couch.

"I'm going to Jess's," I reply quietly, not wanting to say anything to upset him.

It's been the same for the last few days. I get up. I go to Jess's. I eat dinner there, and come home in time for bed, unless there's been a lot of yelling. Then I'll stay over.

So far I've spent two of the last three nights there.

"What's wrong with your home?" Dad asks with such

spite. His lip is curled up. His eyes are squinted. "You have no idea how lucky you are to have a roof over your head. I didn't have my own room as a kid."

"Sorry," I reply. That's all I seem to say to him anymore. Apologize for not being here. Apologize for being here. Apologize for simply being.

"It's okay, sweetheart." Mom walks into the living room. She's wearing a long-sleeve top even though it's hot and humid outside . . . and inside as well. She must be boiling. We aren't allowed to put the air-conditioning on, so I had to sleep with a fan blasting on me last night. I didn't get much sleep between the heat and the shouting.

I force a smile to try to comfort Mom as I turn the corner to leave.

"Wait!" she calls out, but it's too late.

I see it.

Or don't see it.

My piano is gone.

Mom rushes over and puts her arm around me. "Honey, I was about to tell you—"

I shrug her arm off me. "Where did my piano go?" I feel tears burn behind my eyes.

"I sold it," Dad says with meaningful glee in his voice. "I bought it. I can sell it."

"Someone came this morning to pick it up," Mom begins to explain.

At least I know what this morning's fight was about.

My chin twitches, but I don't want my dad to see me cry. It would just make him madder. "How am I supposed to practice?"

"How am I supposed to feed you?" Dad replies in a high and whiny voice.

He *hasn't* been feeding me. I've been having breakfast, lunch, and dinner at the Millers'. Her parents now expect me there. They set a place for me and everything. Mrs. Miller even sets out an afternoon snack for me. I don't know if Mom said something to them, but there seems to be some kind of understanding.

Jess is ecstatic about the arrangement. Being around her is the only thing that makes all of this bearable. But it would be better if I didn't have to keep secrets from her. About my dad's temper. About the baby. I told her my mom wasn't sick anymore, which was true. But when she starts showing, Jess will know I kept it from her.

I open my mouth to reply to Dad, but Mom shakes her head. I understand. It's a warning. I'm not supposed to challenge him. It'll make things worse.

"Things are going to be okay, sweetheart. Your father is going on an interview to work at that big, fancy SuperMart store opening up next month. Right, Frank?"

Dad grumbles something in reply.

People in town are divided over the massive store coming

in right outside the city limits. Either they're thrilled they have all this selection at a discount or they're worried what effect it would have on the small shops downtown.

I'm for whatever will get my dad out of the house.

"Listen," Mom says as she tucks a strand of hair behind my ear. "I was thinking it might be good for you and me to go visit your grandmother. Just for a few days. We can get out of your father's hair. Wouldn't that be fun?"

I nod because that's all I can do.

I usually hate to spend any time away from Jess. Her parents even took me with them to Wisconsin Dells last summer. Jess and I had the best time riding all the waterslides at Noah's Ark and playing mini golf.

As much as I don't want to leave her, it's probably for the best to get away. Even for a little while.

CHAPTER SEVENTEEN

There's a knock on my bedroom door, and to my surprise it's Jackson.

"Oh, hey," I reply. "Is it time to leave?"

I look at the clock on my phone and see we aren't supposed to head out for the Fourth of July festivities for twenty more minutes.

"No, ah." Jackson brushes the bangs from his eyes. "Um, I just wanted to see how you're doing." He kicks at the gray hallway carpeting.

"I'm fine," I reply, even though I don't know if that's the truth.

I've basically been pulling a Jackson the last two days since my fight with Lily. I've hardly left my room. Not like I have anybody to hang out with anyway since Lucas is at his dad's for the holiday. I'm back to being all alone.

Jackson shifts on his feet. He's got on his usual outfit for the rare occurrence when he ventures out of the house: baggy jeans and a baggy black T-shirt with some kind of logo. Today's it's a gray Batman one.

"It's just, like, I know we don't talk that much," he starts.

That's the truth. We don't have that kind of relationship where we have big talks. His face is usually buried in his phone, or he's playing online with his friends. Although in fairness to Jackson, I was usually out with my friends, too.

Was.

"And well . . . the wall between our rooms isn't that thick. And I heard you the other day with Lily . . ." Jackson's pale cheeks are super red. It's something that happens when he's embarrassed.

"Oh, I . . ." My stomach turns when I think about Lily. And today makes it even harder.

Back in my old life, I spent every Fourth of July with Lily's family at her grandparents' lake house in Northern Wisconsin.

That was then. And now . . .

"And like," Jackson continues, still staring down at the floor, "I know I'm quiet and stuff, but I pay attention. And I realize it must be hard for you."

"It is," I admit. I get up and hand my phone to Lucas so he can see the text Lily sent me this morning wishing me a happy Fourth.

He studies it. "At least she's texting you, right?"

I guess.

"Who is she with?" he asks.

Lily had sent me a picture of her on the deck with Shoshanna and another girl I don't recognize but can only assume is the infamous Callie.

The new girl.

My replacement.

"Her friends," I reply, trying to keep my voice even.

Yes, it *is* good we're texting. After our fight, she sent me a picture of our soccer trophy and the caption, "Remembering the good times."

Then yesterday—after I'd cooled off some—I replied with a picture of strawberry shortcake ice cream. I went to Frannie's in an attempt to cheer myself up and thought of Lily when I saw her favorite flavor.

I guess we're now down to a text a day.

Is this how friendships end?

Maybe I don't need to uncover the secrets of Melissa and Jessica's box to understand.

"Uh, can I come in?" Jackson asks. It's then I notice he'd been avoiding stepping inside my room.

"Are you like a vampire or something and need my permission?"

He takes a few hesitant steps in and looks around my room. "This is cool. I like all the pictures and stuff." He goes over to the wall and studies the photos I put up of my old life. Now being surrounding by memories is just depressing, and I think I should take it all down. Maybe start from scratch. Take pictures of my friends here. So basically it would be a Lucas shrine. Which he, no doubt, would love.

"And your trophies." Jackson picks up one of the dozens of soccer trophies that line my bookshelf.

I appreciate Jackson making an effort. Maybe I should try as well. "How has the move been treating you?"

He shrugs. "It's okay. We'll see when I have to start high school, but I figure every school has to have its misfits and gamers." He crosses his fingers.

"Yeah. You seem to be hanging out with your friends just the same as before," I say, trying to not let the jealousy creep into my voice.

Jackson plops down on the bed next to me. "The benefits of virtual friendships, I guess. So, ah, I just want to say that, like, I think you're doing fine. For what it's worth."

Fine? I'm losing Lily. I'm stuck on a couple of items in the box. And with Lucas away, I have zero friends.

If that's *fine*, I don't want to know Jackson's definition of bad.

He laughs lightly. "Yeah, okay, so, like, Peyton, we'd been here for, what, like two days and you made a friend? Lucas is pretty cool. You've never had trouble making friends. It's something I've always been kind of jealous about."

This surprises me. I never thought Jackson would ever be jealous of me.

"Don't let it get to your ego or anything."

Jackson rubs my head playfully while I swat his hand away, but it does bring a smile to my face. He hasn't done that in a really long time.

"And, like, I know you're frustrated with Mom being gone—and yeah, it's a lot—but you used to be the one in the family who was always off with Lily or doing something with the soccer team," Jackson says. "So now just because *you're* the one with more time for the family, you kind of can't get mad that Mom's basically doing what you used to do, except it's for her job."

Huh, he does have a point. "Fair enough," I reply.

What is it with the dudes in my life—first Lucas and now Jackson—making sense? But still, Mom dragged us here, so she could at least make some effort to help us all get adjusted instead of going MIA.

Jackson clears his throat. "Plus, this town isn't that bad."

"Jackson, how much of Lake Springs have you seen?" As far as I know he hasn't really left his bedroom.

"Fair enough," he replies with a wink. "But you seem to like the town. At least you're out with Lucas enough. Why don't you tell me about your favorite places, and maybe you could show me around sometime?"

Hanging out with Jackson? In public? By choice? Honestly, it's not something I ever saw him wanting to do.

And I'm surprised about how much I'm looking forward to it.

My mind begins to race as I think about all the places to take Jackson, which are pretty much the exact sites Lucas showed me.

"Jackson, my favorite sibling—" I begin.

"Your only sibling," Jackson adds.

"Exactly!" I pat him on the back. "What are your thoughts on delicious cheeseburgers, followed by more Frannie's ice cream?"

"Fun fact: that combination is one of the things I'm willing to leave the house for," he says with a smile.

So cheeseburgers and ice cream with Jackson. And we're not being forced into it.

Maybe Lake Springs still has some surprises up its sleeve.

"We're here," Mom says thirty minutes later as she pulls into her faculty parking space at Great Lakes College.

Dad, Mom, Jackson, and I make our way over to the quad where people have blankets sprawled out on the lawn. There are food trucks parked nearby. A brass band is setting up on the steps of one of the buildings. Later tonight they'll be some fireworks.

Got to be honest, my expectations are low. The ones at the lake were nearly twenty minutes long and lit up the entire sky. Everything here is smaller.

"Peyton, I think Madison will be here with her parents and friends," Mom tells me.

I reply with a groan.

"Now Peyton, it's good to make some effort."

"Some effort?" I snap. "Mom, she was rude."

She huffs in return. "I just don't think you gave her a chance."

"Drop it, Shannon," Dad says sternly. I told him everything when he picked me up. I know it makes it difficult for my mother to have her children not get along with another faculty member's kids, but I will not sell out Lucas.

"Mom, let's be real; Peyton's the only one out of us who has made any effort in Lake Springs," Jackson states.

Mom looks stunned that Jackson not only would stand up for me, but also that he's looking up from his phone. For a whole minute before he returns to it.

Baby steps.

We lay out a blanket and the food we brought: cheese, sausage, crackers, fruit salad, and chips. Dad opens the cooler and hands me a water, while Jackson unfolds the chairs.

Once we all sit down, even Mom and Dad get on their phones. So much for family bonding.

"Shannon!" a guy calls out. He's older and has some little kids trailing behind him who I can only guess are his grandchildren. "So glad you could make it."

Mom stands up and motions for us to do the same.

"Yes, thank you, Dean Gibson. We're thrilled to be here."
Mom introduces us to the head of the Political Science
Department.

"Your mother has been such a wonderful addition to the
faculty," he says as Mom stands up a bit straighter next to
him. "All of the English Department has been raving about
the changes she's making."

"Thanks, it's been a lot of work, but it'll be worth it." She
gives us a small, hopeful smile.

That's when it hits me: this has been a big adjustment for
her, too.

Jackson's right. I should cut her some more slack.

"And how's that house working out for you?" he asks.

"It's wonderful. We're still settling in," she replies. All the
boxes have technically been unpacked, but I think it's going
to take a lot longer for us to feel like it's truly our home.

He looks out at the people gathering in the quad. "I have
so many wonderful memories of that house. We could've
stayed, but with the kids gone, there wasn't really any reason
to have all that room."

Wait a second.

"You used to live in our house?" I get a glimmer of hope.

"Why, yes. It's a great place."

"How long did you live there? Were you there in 1989?" I
ask, even though he doesn't really look like an older version of
the guy in the photo—this guy has hair, for one. Although,

the photo guy could've been one of Melissa's uncles or a friend of her parents.

Mom furrows her brow. "I'm sorry, Dean Gibson, Peyton usually isn't this inquisitive. Honestly, she's been a little quiet since we moved here. I guess it's good she's coming out of her funk."

I'm right here! I want to scream. I hate when adults talk about you like you're not there.

He laughs. "That's entirely okay. I like it when kids are interested in history, especially one that's tied to them. But I moved into that house in, let's see . . . It was the early nineties. I can't remember the exact date."

"Oh." I feel defeated. Unless . . . "Who did you buy it from?"

He taps his finger on his chin. "Oh, wow. It was a while ago, but the previous owner fell on a bit of a rough time, which is a shame, especially when kids are involved. When we got the house it had seen better days. We redid the kitchen before we even moved in. And then we did the renovation to add the third bedroom over the garage."

"That's Jackson's bedroom, which is—" Mom begins, but I cut her off.

"Do you remember the previous owner's name? Even the last name?"

Mom gives me a pointed look. "Oh, I don't think—"

"Linda!" Dean Gibson calls out across the yard and waves

a woman over. "My wife has a better memory with things like names."

As an older woman with graying hair approaches us, I get a jolt of excitement with every step. She has no idea how much remembering a name from thirty years ago would mean to me.

"Hello!" she greets us warmly, and Mom forces us to do another round of introductions.

I'm getting impatient as my parents make small talk. Do they not understand how close I am to potentially solving a mystery?

Well, no, because they don't know about the box, but still.

"Excuse me, Mrs. Gibson," I say in the most polite and not at all impatient voice I can muster. "Do you happen to recall who you bought your house from?"

My leg is jostling around with nervous energy. It's like I'm getting ready for kickoff.

"Oh, why yes. It was a Mr. . . . Davis, yes. Frank Davis."

WE HAVE A LAST NAME!

"Did he have a daughter named Melissa or Jessica?"

She grimaces. "Oh, dear, I never met his family."

"Was he white or Asian?"

She gives me an odd look. "Well, he was white," Mrs. Gibson replies.

It's Melissa's dad! Melissa Davis!

WE HAVE A FULL NAME!

Mrs. Gibson continues, "Even though I never met his family, when we toured the house it was very clear a girl lived in an upstairs bedroom at the top of the stairs. There were floor-to-ceiling photos of some boy."

"He was from New Kids on the Block!" I shout. "Probably Joey McIntyre!"

"Peyton!" Mom's jaw is practically on the grass. "What are you talking about? How do you know about New Kids and Joey McIntyre? They're from my generation."

I ignore her. "Thank you!" I say as I jump up and down and unexpectedly hug the woman.

"You're welcome," she replies with a laugh. "I've seen him around town from time to time."

Oh my goodness, oh my goodness, oh my goodness!

Frank Davis is still in Lake Springs.

This is exactly what we need to go forward.

I pull out my phone and text Lucas: "WE HAVE A BREAK!"

We're going to find Melissa's dad.

CHAPTER EIGHTEEN

1989

"This is going to be the best Fourth of July ever!" Jess declares the next afternoon as we wait for the parade to start.

I try to swallow down my feelings as I simply nod along.

Jess holds my hand. "I know, I'm so bummed you're leaving, but it's only for a few days."

"Yeah."

Jess tilts her head at me. "Are you feeling okay? You've been so quiet lately, and it makes me sad." She juts her lip out.

"My stomach hurts." Which is the truth. It started hurting yesterday morning, after the piano incident and Mom telling me about leaving town for a bit. But now it's the only thing I'm looking forward to. Tomorrow afternoon can't come soon enough.

"Do you want to tell my dad? Maybe he can help?" Jess's eyebrows are knitted with concern.

"It's okay." Even though it isn't. I don't think there's any kind of medicine that will help.

"Promise me you'll send a postcard," Jess says. "I'm so mad long-distance phone calls costs so much. I don't know what I'm going to do if we can't talk. I guess I'll just have to put New Kids on repeat. Only Jordan can save me now!" She places her hand on her head dramatically.

I try to force a smile.

Not even Joey McIntyre could make things better.

Which is really saying something.

"Oh, it's starting!" Jess jumps up and down. She breaks out her camera and snaps away as a guy dressed as Uncle Sam walks by on stilts.

I'm grateful for the parade. Jess is focused on all the people passing, so she won't notice how numb I'm feeling to it all.

"Look what I got you girls," Dr. Miller says as he hands us red-and-blue snow cones.

"Daddy, Mel's stomach hurts."

"Oh no." Dr. Miller bends down and puts the back of his hand against my forehead. "You don't feel warm, so it's hopefully not the flu. Is it a sharp or dull pain?"

"I'm okay," I lie.

All I do these days is lie. Isn't keeping something from someone the same as lying?

He frowns. "Well, let me know if you need anything. We'll get you some ginger ale and saltines when we get back to the house. Have to get you ready for the big barbeque."

"We got so much food!" Jess says as she takes a huge bite of the snow cone, her lips staining red and blue.

"Awesome," I reply unenthusiastically.

I usually love parties at the Millers'. They have a huge backyard. They decorate it with lights and streamers. They put out a Slip 'N Slide for us to run down when it's hot. Our attempts at convincing them to get an aboveground pool have continued to be unsuccessful; that's the only thing that would make our summers even better.

Although, I don't think anything can save this summer.

"Dad! Take our picture!" Jess says as she hands him her camera. She flings her arm around me, and I do my best to smile, but it isn't just my stomach.

My whole self hurts.

I'm still in a haze two hours later in the Millers' backyard.

"Are your parents coming?" Jess asks me.

I shake my head. Dad doesn't go to things like this. Mom doesn't do things he doesn't like when he's around. And now he's always around.

She nudges me. "Too bad. I guess I'm just left to have my parents embarrass me. I mean, look at my dad's shorts!" Jess cringes as she points at her father, who is standing in front of the grill with red, white, and blue checkered shorts with a flag T-shirt.

She takes a photo of him and her mom while I swallow the bitterness that's creeping up whenever I think of Jess's parents. She has stability. She has a father who loves her. Who doesn't scare her. I'd trade my father for Jess's any day.

Dr. Miller flips a hamburger in the air, spins around to catch it, but the burger flops to the ground.

"Oh my gosh," Jess says as she covers her face. "My dad is the absolute worst! Right?"

I don't know what to say.

He's not the worst. He's the opposite of being the worst.

He loves Jess. He doesn't yell at her. He doesn't yell at her mother.

"Mel?" Jess tilts her head, then laughs. "Oh my gosh, you're like totally horrified by my dad, right?"

I'm having trouble breathing.

The weight of everything I'm holding in has become too much.

This whole perfect scene with the perfect Millers has become too much.

I do the only thing I can think to do: walk away.

I need to get away from these thoughts that are swirling around in my head.

"Mel?" Jess calls after me.

I get inside the house and am confronted by several pairs of eyes. Friends of the Millers. Fathers who probably have jobs and don't scare their wives and children.

"Mel?"

I run up the stairs to Jess's bedroom. Her pristine bed-room with new sheets and new clothes and new everything.

"Mel?"

I spin around, not sure what to do or where to go. I can't be here anymore. I don't want to go home.

There's an anger bubbling up inside me. Of all the things I don't have. Will never have.

And not just things like nice clothes and new furniture.

"What's going on?" Jess enters her room. She bites her lip.

"Your dad is not the worst!" I yell at her. Even I'm taken aback by the anger in my voice.

Jess recoils. "What?"

I kneel beside her bed and pull out the "K" encyclopedia she has hidden. I hold it up. "You focus on who your parents could be, but they're right down there. They aren't in some book."

"What?" Jess repeats herself, her mouth hung open in shock. "I can't believe you'd say that to me. You're the only one who knows about the encyclopedia." Her bottom lip starts to quiver.

I can't believe I'm doing this to her either. I know I'm being awful, but I can't stop this heaviness in my chest. My entire body is buzzing with frustration and anger.

"You also know how much I want to know where I come from." Tears are now streaming down her face.

I do know. I said that on purpose to hurt Jess. My best

friend. I should apologize and comfort her. That was a horrible thing to say, but I'm just so angry.

So very, very angry.

"Why are you so mad at me?" Jess folds her arms, her sadness turning into frustration.

I don't have an answer, so I stay silent.

"All I've been is nice and a good friend to you, and you've been sullen and mopey, and you won't even talk to me. You're ruining the party!"

"Oh, well, I'm just *soooooo* sorry I'm ruining your perfect party with your perfect family and their perfect fancy friends! I guess I'll just leave." I stomp toward her door.

"No, stop!" Jess calls out. "Just tell me what I did wrong?"

I hate that we're fighting, but I'm too mad at the world, and I need someone to take it out on.

Just like Dad does to us.

"Everything!" I snap.

Jess looks stunned. "Why are you being like this? I thought you were my best friend."

"Yeah, well, maybe we aren't really best friends, then."

My heart breaks as I say it, but I want someone else to hurt as much as I hurt right now.

Jess goes to her bedroom door and opens it. "Then I guess you should go."

I pause, knowing I should fix this. But I don't know how.

"Yeah," I reply in her cool tone. "See ya."

"Have fun with your grandmother."

"Oh, I will." I push my shoulders back. "I'll have THE BEST time."

Even though I won't. I hate being away from Jess. Why can't I just tell her that? Why am I so mad at her?

Jess narrows her eyes at me. "Yeah, well, I'm sure Amy and I will have a great time, too. I bet she'll love getting burgers at Kitchen Corner. Maybe we'll get some magazines at Book World."

I push the jealousy down. I know she's only saying these things to get a reaction from me.

"Well, I guess it's a good thing I'm leaving then."

"Yeah. I guess it is."

Time apart from Jess is the absolute last thing I want. I don't know how things got so bad. All I do know is that it's my fault. But it's too late to fix it.

Maybe a break will be a good thing for us. We'll have time to cool down. I'll come back, and Dad will have a job, and everything will return to normal.

"Yeah, good." I give her a nod as I walk out of her room.

I keep my head down as I leave the Millers' house and don't look up until I get to the safety of my bedroom.

I close the door and break down in tears.

I've messed everything up.

CHAPTER NINETEEN

We found Frank Davis.

It was so easy. Just one quick search, and we discover he's at the Phoenix, a senior assisted living facility in town.

Melissa was not so simple. An online search came up with thousands of Melissa Davises. We narrowed it to the Minneapolis–St. Paul area, and over a dozen people showed up, two without photos.

I felt a little defeated, but it doesn't really matter. We don't need the internet to find her. We have her father.

We're getting so close.

Ms. Ryan parks the van in front of the Phoenix, a three-story apartment building near downtown that takes up an entire block. I've passed it a bunch of times.

He's been here all along.

Lucas's mom hands us a container of brownies she made.

"Stress baking," Lucas explained to me last night. "It's

the whole allowing her beloved, frail child to talk to strangers thing."

"You're not frail," I had said.

"Oh, don't I know it. Maybe someday she'll come around to that fact."

Now Ms. Ryan opens the van door. "Are you ready?" she asks in a chipper voice.

I've never been so ready. I could hardly sleep last night I was so excited to find out more about Melissa.

She glances at her watch. "Right on time! When I called, the office manager said Mr. Davis doesn't get many visitors, poor thing."

Melissa must live outside the Minneapolis area if she doesn't see her dad that much.

Lucas uses the van's ramp to get to the sidewalk. "Thanks, Mom."

She wrings her hands. "I really feel like I should come in. He wasn't very friendly on the phone."

But he did agree to let us visit him.

That's all we need. I'm sure when he finds out what we have, he'll be really excited, too.

"Mom," Lucas says firmly. "We are entering one of the few places on this planet where I'll be able to outmaneuver the majority of people inside. Let me have my moment." He puffs out his chest.

Ms. Ryan looks back and forth between Lucas and the entrance of the building.

The front door opens, and an elderly woman is pushing an equally old man in a wheelchair.

"See!" Lucas says. "I'm with my people!"

Ms. Ryan doesn't look entirely convinced, but then she takes a step back. "I'll be waiting in the van. All you have to do is text, and I'll come running."

"With the cavalry, I'm sure," Lucas says dryly. Then he takes his mom's hand. "But thanks, Mom. I appreciate it."

She brushes her hand against his cheek. "I just want you to be safe."

I turn away from this personal moment to focus on the building in front of us. We'll finally get some answers inside. We can even possibly get Melissa her box and find out what happened with her and Jessica. She'll probably be so happy to have it back with all the amazing memories it brings.

We approach the front and buzz the door. As we enter, we're greeted by a woman behind a front desk.

"Hello, I'm Peyton Howard and this is Lucas Ryan. We're here to see Frank Davis." I feel so grown up getting to come in here by ourselves.

The woman gives us a confused look before typing into the computer. "Did you talk to Frank?"

"My mother did," Lucas explains.

It's true Mr. Davis was a bit rude, but he was also very confused about why we'd want to meet with him. I mean, it would actually be really weird if he was totally cool with two random kids coming in. Then, she mentioned I lived in his old house and found something that might belong to him, and he said okay.

So here we are.

The receptionist gives us a hesitant smile as she flags over a woman in a nursing uniform. "Hey, Clara. These two are here to see Frank."

Clara stops in her tracks. "Well, look at that, Frank has a visitor."

I feel bad for Mr. Davis that nobody comes and visits him. It must be really lonely. Though as I look around the bright entryway with a bulletin board filled with lists of activities and photographs, I realize that he can't be too lonely being surrounded by so many people.

"Come along, I'll take you to Frank's room." Clara motions for us to follow her.

Lucas weaves around the giant hallway. "Look at this place. It's amazing. Wide hallways and doors. Maybe I should live here. Hey, Clara, what's the age requirement for a sweet spot here?"

She laughs in response, while I can feel my heart start beating faster with every step.

This is it.

I think back to less than three weeks ago when Dad told me to dig up the weeds. I was miserable. I was bored. I didn't know anybody. *I* was lonely.

So much has happened since then—including making a friend in Lucas—and it's all due to Frank's daughter.

We arrive at room 107. Clara knocks on the door. "Frank, your visitors are here!" she says brightly as she opens the door.

Mr. Davis is hunched over in a reclining chair that looks out of the window. He turns and regards us for a moment before looking back. He's bald with strands of white hair around the side of his head. He's wearing jeans and a long-sleeve shirt. I picture the younger guy in the barbeque photo; they don't look much alike. Maybe it wasn't Melissa's dad.

His living room, with a small kitchenette in the corner, is sparse. There isn't any personality. No photos. Nothing.

I can't help but feel sad for Mr. Davis. It looks like it's a lonely life.

"Frank, did you hear me?" Clara asks a little louder.

He nods. "What do you want?" he asks gruffly.

"Now, Frank, be nice." Carla comes over to Mr. Davis and straightens out the blanket on his lap.

Mr. Davis is ten years younger than my grandfather, who seems to have a lot more energy.

Poor Mr. Davis.

"Hi, Mr. Davis," I start, but his attention shifts to Lucas.

"You're a cripple," he states flatly.

Never mind. Melissa's dad is kind of a jerk.

For the first time since I've known Lucas, he's quiet.

"Frank!" Clara shakes her head. "These two kids came to visit you. Where are your manners?"

He grunts back in response.

"You'll have to excuse Frank. He doesn't get many visitors, and now I can see why." She walks over to the front door, leaning against it. "I'll stay here for your chat."

I look around the apartment, wondering if I should sit down. Since Mr. Davis hasn't said anything about making myself comfortable, I remain standing.

"Hi, I'm Peyton. I live in your old house at 247 Maple," I begin to explain.

"That dump," he replies.

I want to protest. I don't know what the house was like when he lived here, but it's nice now. At least we're trying to make the best of it.

Wait a second. When did I start becoming positive about life in Lake Springs?

Whoa.

"Yes, well," I recover. "I was doing some yard work when we moved in, and I found something that I believe belonged to your daughter, Melissa."

I hold my breath as I wait for Mr. Davis to fill us in on the person we've been chasing the last couple of weeks.

He finally turns his head and looks at me. "Who?"

No. I thought . . .

"Melissa?" I say again.

He stares blankly at me.

I reach into my back pocket and produce the photo of Melissa and Jessica that was in the box. The box remains in my backpack, as I don't trust him with it. Yet.

I hand him the photo. He holds on to it with shaking hands.

His face gets red as he studies the photograph. His breathing deepens.

"You okay, Frank?" Clara calls out.

He takes the photograph and crumples it in his hands.

"Hey!" Lucas calls out. He moves his wheelchair so it's between Mr. Davis and me.

Mr. Davis clenches the photo in his balled-up fist. "I don't have a daughter."

"But—" I begin, but stop myself.

He had lived in that house. He had a daughter.

"Or was Jessica your daughter?" I ask. She could've been adopted.

He throws the photograph down on the floor. "I have no daughter."

This wasn't how this was supposed to go, but I certainly can't argue with someone over whether or not he has a kid.

Maybe he has Alzheimer's? Shoshanna's grandmother has it; a person with the disease forgets a lot about their lives.

Or maybe something horrible happened to Melissa. And here we come bringing up painful memories.

"Did you ever have any kids?" I ask cautiously, but Mr. Davis refuses to look at me.

"We should leave," Lucas says under his breath.

I can only nod as I quickly pick up the photo before we move toward the door.

"I'm sorry if I upset you," I say. Or maybe we have this all wrong. Maybe he always wanted kids and I brought up a sore subject.

But there's also a part of me that thinks that maybe Mr. Davis is lying to us.

He changed when he saw that photo. He became angry. You don't respond that way looking at a picture of a stranger.

"I'm so sorry," Clara says as she closes Frank's apartment door behind us. "Frank hasn't ever had any family visit. I have no idea if he has any kids, to be honest. As you could see, he doesn't have the sunniest disposition."

No kidding.

This time, as I walk down the hallway, I feel so defeated. None of it makes sense.

"I thought we were so close," I say to Lucas.

"We were," he replies, equally defeated.

We leave the complex, and Lucas's mom appears surprised to see us so soon.

She gets out of the van. "How was it?"

Neither Lucas nor I know what to say.

She notices the batch of brownies in Lucas's lap.

"You didn't give him the brownies?"

Lucas looks down at the container as if he forgot it was there. "He doesn't deserve your brownies." He then opens it up and helps himself to one. He holds it out for me. "She gave them the nut-free treatment."

So I take one. And it's perhaps the best brownie I've ever had: rich, gooey, with some salted caramel swirled on top.

Lucas was right: Mr. Davis doesn't deserve something so delicious.

"But, Lucas," his mom begins.

"Mom, he called me . . ." But Lucas doesn't say the word. And no way am I going to.

"What?" Ms. Ryan asks. "What did he say to you?" Anger rises in her voice.

"Mr. Davis is kind of mean," I explain.

"I should go in there right now and—"

"Let's just leave," Lucas says as he gets inside the van.

I also want to get as far away from Frank Davis as possible.

Yet again, I feel defeated. I have no idea what to do next. Maybe we'll never find Melissa or Jessica. Maybe we'll never know what happened.

"Now what?" I ask once we're settled into the van.

"There's only one option left." Lucas opens the box and pulls out the note with the code. "We have to crack this thing."

CHAPTER TWENTY

1989

I can't get out of bed the next morning.

I throw my covers over my head to block out the sunlight that is peaking through the windows. I don't want to wake up and be reminded of what happened yesterday.

Not like I got any sleep.

Yesterday was THE WORST. The absolute WORST.

There's a light knock on my bedroom door.

"Melissa, honey." Mom opens the door a little and sticks her head in. "Everything okay?"

I reply by turning over so my back is to her.

I can tell that she sits on my bed because I feel her beside me. She places her hand on my back.

"Jessica came by."

This gets my attention. I sit up and look at Mom. She's got an orange Nike shoebox in her lap. Jess wrote our names in her swirly cursive and put a bunch of stickers on the box.

"She wanted me to give this to you." Mom brushes my hair with her hand. "I take it you got into a fight. These things happen. Just know that everything is going to be okay. *We* are going to be okay, Melissa. I promise."

I nod. If Jess stopped by, this must mean that she hasn't entirely given up on me.

Not that I don't deserve it after my outburst yesterday.

Like father, like daughter.

But no. I won't be like my dad. Ever.

I'll apologize and make it up to Jess.

As Mom stands, she stretches her hands above her head. I get a peek of her stomach. It's got a little bit of a bump.

Dad is going to find out soon.

He's going to get so angry. I didn't think it was possible for things to get worse, but I have a feeling they will.

"Why don't you start packing a bag for your grandmother's?" Mom says as she goes into my closet and pulls out my blue duffel bag.

I finally sit up and nod. "Okay."

"There's my girl," Mom says with a small, sad smile.

Once she closes the door behind her, I open up the box. It has a bunch of items we were going to put in our time capsule. There's a note inside.

Mel, I don't like how we left things. I'm still upset, but you're my best friend. Here's a reminder of how totally awesome our summer has been. I took the last of the pictures yesterday, including one just for you. See you in a week. Love, Jess

I hug the letter tightly to my chest. We'll be okay. I just know it.

I look through the box and see the film we're supposed to get developed, along with Teddy. She wants me to take care of him. But really we both know that Teddy will look after me. I smile as I go through so many of our memories. When I get back, we'll still have almost two months to add to the box.

I'm going to send Jess a postcard every day while I'm at Grandma's, and we can put them in here.

Her note is the first thing I pack into my duffel bag.

We can still have a great summer, maybe even the best. We just have to wait a few days.

I finish packing, but I still don't feel right.

Mom didn't say when we're leaving, so I should have enough time to bike to Jess's to apologize to her and make sure we're going to be okay.

I start heading downstairs, but I pause when I see Dad standing near the front door.

Another reason I didn't sleep was because things got really bad last night. I heard something break in the middle of one of his yelling fits, but nothing looks broken.

Not like the house is the same since he sold my piano. There's a big gap here. It feels a little less like home.

Maybe my future baby brother or sister will help fill the holes that Dad keeps poking into our family.

Dad looks Mom up and down. "I probably won't be back until you leave. Call me when you get to your mother's."

"Will do." Mom is giving Dad a big smile. It's the first genuine one I've seen from her in a while. I'm sort of mad that she smiles at him after he's been so mean to her. "Have a great time with your friends."

He gives Mom a kiss on the cheek and heads out the door without saying goodbye to me.

Good. I didn't want to have to pretend like I was going to miss him anyways.

Mom stands at the front door and waves at Dad. She stays there smiling at him until his truck is out of her eyesight.

She turns around and sees me.

"Do I have time to—" I begin, but Mom comes running toward me.

"We have to move!" She grabs my hand and leads me quickly upstairs. "Pack as much as you can. Only clothes and necessities."

"What? I already packed."

She throws open my closet door and starts taking out clothes by the bunch and throwing them on my bed. She opens up my drawers and does the same.

I watch her in shock.

"I don't need all of these clothes. Why would I need sweaters?"

"We're leaving!" Mom says, her voice high.

"I know we're—"

"No!" Mom bends down in front of me so we're nearly eye to eye. "I need you to listen very carefully, Melissa. We have to leave your father. That means we're packing as much as we can and getting out before he returns. I'm sorry to do this to you, but it's the only way we can escape him."

"What do you mean? We're not going to Grandma's?" None of this makes sense.

"Honey, we are going to live with Ceci. It's not safe to be here anymore."

"For how long?"

Mom looks anguished. "For good."

"What? But Cecilia lives hours away. What about Jess?"

"I'm so sorry, honey. We have to do this. For you. For the baby. For me."

"No!" I push myself away from Mom, and she gasps from pain as she grabs her wrist. The sleeve lifts up, and I can see a big bruise. "What happened?"

"Melissa, I've tried to protect you, but it's getting harder and harder. It's not safe to be here anymore. So you have to trust me. We have to go *now*."

Mom shoves my clothes on the bed into a suitcase while I stand there trying to figure out what this all means. I've been spending more time away from home, and things with Dad have gotten really bad, but she can't mean we're leaving Lake Springs for good.

I move toward the stairs. "I have to tell Jess."

"No." Mom pulls me in a tight embrace. "I know this is hard for you to understand, but we can't tell anybody, Melissa. Nobody can know where we're going. It's the only way to be safe from your father."

Another secret. The first one nearly ruined my friendship.

"But she's my best friend."

Tears begin to flood Mom's eyes. "I'm not saying that you can't eventually contact her, but we need to leave without anybody realizing that we're not coming back. And this also protects Jessica, honey. You want her to be safe from your father, right?"

Of course.

I picture my dad beating on Jess's front door. Him shouting. Him accusing her. She's a horrible liar.

Not like me.

I have to protect my best friend.

"But I can contact her in a little bit?" I ask. "When we know Dad's not looking for us anymore?"

"Yes, but I don't want to lie to you. It might not be for a while. What we need to focus on right now is for you to pack so we can leave right away."

She runs out of my room and starts going up and down

the stairs, carrying luggage and plastic bags. I'm still in shock as I look at my room, unsure the next time I'm going to be here.

I see the Nike box on my bed. I can't just leave without Jess knowing what happened to me.

An idea springs into my head. I'll send Jess a postcard that simply tells her to find the box. She'd be the only one who'll understand what that means. I can bury the box—and the secret—for her to find.

I take a marker from my desk and write "I'm so sorry. Please forgive me." on the inside lid of the box so she knows right away how sorry I am.

Now, I need to figure out a way for her to find me. I can't write her a normal letter since Dad could find it.

The code.

Last summer Jess and I made up a secret code. I take out a piece of paper and write it down. It's so simple Jess will remember it as soon as she sees the note. She'll understand what it means.

I pause as I try to figure out what to say to her. How could I possibly explain all of this?

I look in the mirror and see my reflection. The best friend necklace. I know exactly what to do. I take it off and add it to the box.

This will work. She'll read the letter, and she'll understand why I had to leave and how to find me.

All she needs to do is find the box.

CHAPTER TWENTY-ONE

FJ KLQ DLFKD QL JV DOXKAJLQEβOP. TβOβ
IβXSFKD JV AXA. FQP DLQQβK YXA. FJ KLQ
XIILTβA QL ZXII VLR, YRQ FSβ IβCQ JV
KβZHIXZβ CLO TEβK Tβ PββB βXZE LQEβO
XDXFK. FII Yβ XQ JV JLJP YβPQ COFβKAP
ELRPβ, ZβZFIFX MXIRZEKFXH FK TXRTXQLPX, TF.
ZLJβ CFKA Jβ. VLRO YCC, XITXVP.

There had been a lot in the box that was confusing, but this note—whatever it says—is the most.

And it could be the biggest clue. Our only clue left. Our last chance.

No pressure or anything.

Lucas is typing away at his computer. "So, if my suspicions are correct, this is a code where they've shifted the letters by a few spaces. Like if they started with the letter 'A,' it turned into 'B,' which means 'B' turned into 'C,' and so forth. Like this."

Lucas moves his computer screen so I can see.

ABCDEFGHIJKLMNOPQRSTUVWXYZ

CODED TO: BCDEFGHIJKLMNOPQRSTUVWXYZA

So we'd have to go through all the possibilities until we find the right match.

"Luckily, I was able to do a computer program to translate it instantly . . . if we know where the code starts. There are hundreds of possibilities, especially if they didn't use a straight alphabet. But I'll start with 'A' turning into 'B.'"

He waits for the computer to translate, and it's pure gibberish.

"Okay, 'A' turning into 'C.'"

Nothing.

I nod along as I write out the alphabet on a piece of paper.

If Lily and I had a secret code, what would we have done?

I think back to a time when we wanted to do everything together. We didn't like it if we even had a class apart. There was a semester we didn't have lunch together, and it was the worst.

I tap the "L" of the alphabet in front of me. If we wanted

to do a code, what would we have done? Wouldn't I want to have us be as close as possible?

An idea strikes me. What if Melissa and Jessica used their names as the key?

I put an "M" above the "J," so the letter "M" here would *decode* to be "J." If that was the key, what would the rest of the alphabet look like? I begin to work.

DEFGHIJKLM̲NOPQRSTUVWXYZABC

DECODE AS: ABCDEFGHIJ̲KLMNOPQRSTUVWXYZ

In this version, the letter "D" in the code would actually be "A." I begin to decode. The first word is "CG."

So maybe not.

But it would be entirely different if the "J" represented "M" instead.

I do another key.

XYZABCDEFGHIJ̲KLMNOPQRSTUVW

DECODE AS: ABCDEFGHIJKLM̲NOPQRSTUVWXYZ

I feel a bit hopeless as I put together the first word.

"IM"

A feeling of excitement swells in my belly as the next word is "NOT."

"Lucas!" I exclaim. "I think I figured it out."

Lucas looks from his computer to me. "But how? Before the computer."

"Hey, this thing is pretty useful, too." I tap my head.

"It seems that I have underestimated you." Lucas nods with respect.

"Thanks, I—you what?" I didn't realize that was kind of an insult.

"I'm *kidding*." Lucas does this slight eye roll, which I'm becoming more and more familiar with when I don't get his humor. "What do you have?"

"They lined up the alphabet so the 'J' in the coded note is really an 'M.'"

Lucas's eyes get wide. "Because they're best friends."

"So their original key was 'A' turns into 'X.'"

Lucas's fingers fly over his computer. I stand over his shoulder as he hits Enter, and the decoded note appears on his screen.

IM NOT GOING TO MY GRANDMOTHERS. WERE
LEAVING MY DAD. ITS GOTTEN BAD. IM NOT
ALLOWED TO CALL YOU, BUT IVE LEFT MY
NECKLACE FOR WHEN WE SEE EACH OTHER AGAIN.
ILL BE AT MY MOMS BEST FRIENDS HOUSE, CECILIA
PALUCHNIAK IN WAUWATOSA, WI. COME FIND ME.
YOUR BFF, ALWAYS.

Whoa. This is crazy.

It wasn't at all what I imagined. Not like I had any clue, but I didn't think it would be this.

The feeling of excitement has turned sour. This wasn't just a time capsule.

It was a cry for help.

Now what?

This is something I've been thinking a lot.

I pace around the dining room table in Lucas's house. We have all the items from the box spread out on the table.

"Found her!" Lucas exclaims as he searches his laptop. He writes down the phone number for Cecilia Paluchniak. "Thank goodness for uncommon last names."

So now we know where one of the girls went. But which?

"So we're just supposed to call this woman up and ask if someone named Melissa or Jessica came to her house in 1989 because she had to leave her dad?"

Lucas looks thoughtful for a moment. "Well, it has to be Melissa. You met Mr. Davis. He was not a pleasant person."

He had a point.

I study the letter. "She wanted her best friend to come find her, and she never did." My heart hurts thinking about that.

Unless Jessica found the letter, but . . . she couldn't have.

I'm the first person to find this box.

This secret had been buried for years.

"Do you think they ever found each other?"

Lucas shakes his head. "I have no idea. If Melissa moved to Wauwatosa and Jessica had no idea where she went . . ."

"Melissa could've called her or sent her a letter."

"But then wouldn't she have retrieved the box? It has all these items, including the necklace. Melissa wanted Jessica to find this."

So were Melissa and Jessica—two childhood best friends—still out there somewhere not knowing what happened to each other?

"Well, we have the internet now. If they were these best friends, wouldn't they have found each other eventually?"

Lucas nods. "True. Although Melissa Davis was a little hard to find because of her common name. Jessica might have an easier name to track. So, yeah, maybe."

We just don't know for sure.

Again, so now what?

Lucas's mom walks into the dining room, followed by his aunt Amy.

"Hi, guys." Amy studies the table in front of her. "You've got some project here."

"How's it going?" Ms. Ryan asks cautiously. She must know Lucas gets agitated every time she wants to help.

"I think we're almost there," Lucas replies, but I'm not so sure.

"This brings back some memories," Amy remarks as she picks up the New Kids on the Block picture collage.

Lucas's mom looks uncertain. She wrings her hands and opens her mouth, then closes it.

"Yes, Mother?" Lucas asks with his eyebrows raised.

"Now, Lucas, I know you wanted to do this on your own, but I got the photo of the girls from your grandfather's phone and decided to post it online and ask if anybody knew them."

"You did what?" Lucas protests. "I just knew you didn't think I could do something on my own."

"That's not it, sweetheart—"

"No!" Lucas's face gets red. "Ever since the accident you treat me like I'm this breakable thing who can't do anything. I'm still the same person. I can still do a lot of things—"

"I know Jessica and Melissa!" Amy shouts out.

"WHAT?" Lucas and I exclaim in unison.

Ms. Ryan is fighting back tears. "Lucas, I'm so proud of you. And I know about all the things you can do. I didn't post it because I doubted you. I did it because those girls are from my generation, so I thought I'd ask and well . . ."

"Oh, I just assumed . . . ," Lucas says. He looks down at the floor.

"I know I get too worried about you, but do you blame me?" She brushes her hand against his cheek. "I almost lost you once. I'm trying to let go a little, but it's hard."

Lucas doesn't say anything for a beat. He clears his throat. "Yes, well, I am a rather delightful creature to be around, so I can see why it's difficult. Who wouldn't want to spend all their time with me?"

"Exactly." His mom wipes away a stray tear from her face.

"And, well, I'm sorry I jumped down your throat. I know I can also be a little stubborn—"

"Just a little," his aunt adds with a wink.

He grimaces before registering what this all means. "Wait, you know Jessica and Melissa?"

"Well, I guess I should say I *knew* them," she clarifies.

Lucas hits his forehead. "I didn't even think about the fact that you would've been . . ."

"In the same grade."

"You knew Jessica? And Melissa?" I ask, my voice high.

THIS IS HUGE! How did we not ask Amy about this when we saw her at Lucas's grandparents' house? Had we already put the photo away? Did Lucas not ask because he didn't want his mom to know?

You know what? None of that matters now.

We have our break.

Amy sits down next to Lucas. "Yes, we were friends. But then Melissa kind of disappeared one summer. It broke Jessica's heart."

Lucas and I exchange a look.

"Jessica didn't know why Melissa moved?" Lucas asks.

Amy shakes her head. "No. Nobody did. It was a really bad summer for Jessica."

We know why Melissa left.

"Were you close to Jessica?" I ask.

"A little. Nobody could compete with Melissa in Jessica's eyes. They were as close as two friends could be."

"Does she still live here?" I ask. We can bring the box over to Jessica and tell her why Melissa had to leave.

I can't even imagine how much it must hurt to have your friend disappear on you like that.

"No. She moved to a suburb of St. Paul not long after Melissa left."

Lucas isn't the only one who's stunned. "What's her last name?" Lucas has his fingers at the keyboard, ready to find our Jessica.

"Miller."

Lucas throws his head back. "Miller! There's no way I'll be able to find—"

"Her last name is Berardo now. She's married and lives in Hudson, Wisconsin."

We stare at his aunt in shock. Someone had the answers all along. If only we hadn't been so stubborn about asking for help.

Well, if *Lucas* hadn't been so stubborn. No way anybody in my family would've had this information.

Amy holds up a piece of paper. "We're Facebook friends, and, well, I have this."

She sets down a piece of paper with an email address.

We can contact Jessica.

We might be able to find Melissa.

We can fix this.

CHAPTER TWENTY-TWO

Everything was falling into place.

Or so I thought.

Because of course things could never just work out.

Of course not.

"Yikes. This isn't good," Lucas says to me the following week in his living room. We're staring at an email on his computer.

"I think the word you're looking for is *disaster.*" My stomach ties up in knots.

"I mean, at least we finally got a response," Lucas says with a shrug.

"Are you trying to find a bright side to this?" I gesture at the email we got from Jessica.

The Jessica.

After sending a note explaining who we are and that we found the box, we heard nothing. We sent two follow-up emails. A week later, we finally hear back from her.

And it's not the response we were anticipating.

Dear Peyton and Lucas,

While I appreciate your efforts to reach me, I have no interest in seeing the time capsule. I don't need to see what's in it as I'm the one who packed it. To be honest, thinking about that time in my life has brought up some painful memories. You may be too young to understand, but there comes a time when you have to accept that a friendship has run its natural course. Some things are best left in the past.

Best,
Jessica

"That's it?" Lucas says.

"No, it can't be." It just can't be. Then something she wrote hits me. "*Jessica's* the one who packed the time capsule?"

Lucas looks thoughtful for a moment. "Melissa must've added the code before she buried it."

"The coded letter that explains what happened to Melissa. Jessica doesn't know. All this time . . ." I guess I'd be mad, too, if Lily just up and left without a word.

"Maybe we should email her what the letter said; then she'd understand."

"Maybe." I can't believe that Jessica would just throw away a friendship like the one she had with Melissa. That she wouldn't want to know what happened to her best friend. "I think it's best for her to see the box for herself. Like it was supposed to happen back in 1989."

"There's another way to get some answers," Lucas says as he picks up a piece of paper.

"I was hoping we'd have some news for her. *Good news* at least."

I'd been really looking forward to our upcoming conversation, but now . . . For about the billionth time this summer, I feel frustrated, lost, and hopeless.

"Hey, Mom!" Lucas calls out. Ms. Ryan walks into the living room. "It's time."

Ms. Ryan jumps up in excitement, as I begin to nervously pace the room.

"Now remember to not overwhelm her," she reminds us as she dials her phone.

She places it on speaker and lays it on the coffee table.

The phone rings, and I can hardly breathe.

"Hello?" an older woman says.

"Hello!" Lucas practically screams. "It's Lucas! Lucas from ah—"

"Deep breaths," his mom says, even though she's biting her nails.

"Hi, Lucas," the woman replies. "Thanks so much for contacting Cecilia. This is Melissa."

Melissa. THE Melissa!

The girl in the photographs. The one who used to live in my house. The person we've been chasing for weeks.

She's on the phone.

And we don't have any good news to tell her.

"Hi, Melissa!" Lucas says. "I'm here with my friend Peyton. She's the one who found the box you buried."

"Hi!" I say, my voice super high. "I live in your old house."

"Does the second-to-last stair still squeak?" she asks. Her voice sounds light and friendly.

"No." I can't hold in all that I want to know *right this very second*. "Do you remember the box?"

A laugh comes through the phone. "Of course I do! Even though it's been over thirty years, there are some things a best friend never forgets. I can't believe you found our time capsule. I just sort of always hoped . . ."

Lucas and I exchange a look. She had hoped Jessica had found it.

"I don't mean to pry," Lucas begins, but all we want right now from Melissa are some answers. "But in the letter you left behind—"

"I still can't believe you were able to decode it," Melissa says. "When Cecilia told me about your conversation, I was so shocked. You guys are pretty smart."

"Peyton figured it out before my computer," Lucas states proudly.

And I can't help but smile at the compliment.

"But, so . . ." Lucas hesitates. "It seemed that you had to move pretty quickly. Is that why you buried the box?"

Ms. Ryan sits down next to me on the couch. All three of us are leaning toward the phone, hoping to understand what exactly happened back in 1989.

"Yes, it was a last resort. Now I realize how silly it was, but I couldn't really think straight. My mom sprung the move on me so fast," Melissa begins to explain. "I have a better understanding of everything now that I'm an adult. You see, I'm a social worker and deal with similar situations all the time. My father wasn't safe to be around, so I appreciate what my mother did. I was so angry at her back then. But I think there was a part of me that knew we had to leave. As you know from the letter, we moved in with my mom's best friend, but what I didn't know was that we were going to change our last names to my mother's maiden name. I'll admit it was rough for a while, but my younger brother got to grow up away from the shouting and fighting."

It's not surprising that they left because of Mr. Davis. That's why he was so angry when we showed him that photo.

"I wasn't allowed to tell Jess, and it nearly destroyed me." There's a catch in her voice. "You don't have the same kind of friendships like the ones you have when you're a kid. I assumed Jess never found the box, but now I know for sure. And, it's just . . ."

Heartbreaking.

I don't need Melissa to tell me what it feels like to lose a best friend.

I bite my lip as I think about Lily. Lucas reaches out and pats my back. He gives me a smile that reminds me that I'm not alone here in Lake Springs. Far from it.

"Did you . . . ?" I start to ask, but then stop myself. I don't want to pry, but we're talking with someone who has all the answers. "Did you ever reach out to Jessica?"

We hear a small sigh. "I had sent her a postcard in our special code that told her to find the box, but I never heard from her," Melissa says, a sadness in her voice. "You guys might not understand this, but long-distance calls were really expensive when I was a kid. All I wanted for my twelfth birthday was to call Jess. And then when I did, her number was disconnected. So I mailed a letter the next day. It was sent back, return to sender."

My hand flies up to my mouth. No. There had to have been a way to reach her back then.

"What about now? With Facebook?" I ask, because that's how Amy and Jessica keep in touch.

"Jess was the first person I tried to find, but it was useless. There are too many Jessica Millers in the world. Even though my Jess was one in a million. I always hoped that she would find me, but I haven't used Davis as a last name since . . ."

Because she still doesn't want her father to find her.

My throat burns. Melissa has been searching for her all this time.

"To be honest, I always sort of assumed that Jess did get the postcard, but she was too mad at me to find the box. The last time we saw each other, we had this huge fight, so . . ."

Lucas and I look at each other.

Do we tell her? he mouths to me.

I don't want to cause Melissa any more pain. If Jessica knew about Melissa's dad, she had to forgive her.

"Melissa," I say in a confident voice. "We found Jessica."

"You have!" And just like that, joy has returned to Melissa's voice. "Oh wow, I never thought I'd get to talk to her again."

Lucas cringes next to me.

"How often is someone given a second chance?" she continues.

Maybe I shouldn't get her hopes up, but I'm not going to give up on their friendship, even though Jessica has.

Like Melissa said, you never have the same kind of friendships you have when you're a kid.

"Melissa, I promise you that we're going to get Jessica that box."

CHAPTER TWENTY-THREE

"I never thought I'd say this, but I guess there's a benefit to having a mother who likes to get involved," Lucas says as we watch his mom pace back and forth in their living room.

Everything we've done now hangs on Ms. Ryan.

"I completely understand," she's saying into the phone. "And we certainly don't want to bring up any bad memories, but . . . Oh, I see. *Oh*."

Well, that doesn't sound good.

Ms. Ryan nervously twirls her finger around her ponytail. "It's just we really think you'd want to see what's inside of it."

I finally can't take it anymore. "Do you think I could talk to her?"

She nods with relief. I'm not sure how much better I'll fair, but I also know a little something about what it's like to lose a best friend.

"I think it would be best for you to speak with Peyton. Would that be okay?"

My pulse quickens while we wait for an answer.

Ms. Ryan breaks out into a smile and gives me a thumbs-up. "Okay, here you go."

She hands me the phone, and I pause before bringing it to my ear.

This is it.

Weeks of searching and investigating and questioning has come down to right now.

"Thanks for agreeing to speak to me, Dr. Berardo."

"You can call me Jessica." The voice on the other line is of a woman, but I keep picturing her as the girl in the photos, with her long hair in a high ponytail and colorful scrunchie.

"Hi, Jessica."

The person we've been chasing the last few weeks is speaking to me on the phone right now.

All I need is for her to agree to let us give her the box.

"I'm really sorry for bothering you," I say, a slight waver in my voice. "But I just moved this year and have lost my best friend."

It's time I face the facts. Things between Lily and me will never be the same. But what I've discovered from looking at Melissa and Jessica's friendship over thirty years ago is that some friendships may come to an end, but that doesn't mean they weren't special. That they didn't leave an imprint on your heart. I'd never trade away my time with Lily. She was a very important person in my life; she still is. We live too far away for us to have the relationship we once had. And that's okay.

We all move on. She has Callie. I have Lucas.

But at least I know what happened to her.

"And I know the hurt that can happen. For me, it would be even worse if Lily just disappeared and I didn't know what happened to her. I'm sure you've waited a long time to hear from Melissa."

Jessica lets out a breath. "It *has* been a long time, but I can still remember it clearly. I feel like all I did that summer was wait for Mel. I ran to the mailbox every afternoon to see if the postcard she promised me had arrived. Nothing. I waited a week for her to return from her trip. Nothing. I rode my bike past her house every day. Nothing. In the evening, I would sit with the phone in my lap, expecting Mel to call any minute to tell me she was back. Nothing." There's a crack in her voice, just like the one Melissa had. "We got into a huge fight before she left. So then I just assumed that Mel was still mad at me. Before I knew it there was a For Sale sign posted in the front of her yard. My parents told me that they probably moved, but *of course* I would hear from Mel again. *Of course* I would." There's bitterness that's crept into her voice. "We were best friends. But nothing. Always nothing. It still stings"

"I can't even imagine what that was like, which is why I

think you need to know the truth about what happened to Melissa that summer."

There's a pause on the other end of the line. "Is Mel okay?"

The panic in her voice is proof that she still cares.

"Yes."

"Good, but I don't really understand how a box will change things. It really can't make up for thirty years of silence. I'm a different person than I was at eleven, I'm sure she is as well."

We can't make up for the lost time, but the box can at least give her what Lucas's mom calls closure. To have something resolved emotionally.

Jessica isn't the only one who needs some closure.

I think back to all the photos we saw of Melissa and Jessica around Lake Springs. The smiles. The laughter. The kind of bond only two best friends can have.

"It looks like you guys had so much fun," I say to her.

"We really did."

"And because of the box, I've been introduced to the most delicious cheeseburgers in Lake Springs."

"Oh!" she exclaims. "Is Kitchen Corner still around?"

"It's Mimi's Café now."

"*Mimi* is still around?"

"Wait, you know Mimi?" I ask.

"Yes! She was a waitress there back in my day. Mel's mother also worked there sometimes."

Mimi did know them! If only I had shown her the photo. You know, Lucas joked about going door to door, but maybe it would've worked.

Not that it matters now. We have Melissa. We have Jessica. We just need to find a way to get them together.

"How long has it been since you've visited Lake Springs?" I ask.

"I haven't been back since we moved, which was at the end of that summer. It's funny because I protested even the idea of moving earlier, but then when my dad got this big promotion, I was happy to leave. There were too many memories of Mel in Lake Springs."

I can't help but think about all of the memories Lily has of me in every place she goes to. Maybe this move was just as hard on her. I left everything behind, but there aren't any reminders of her here. I got to have a fresh start.

"Did you ever try to find Melissa?" I ask, wondering if Jessica had really given up on her.

"I'd lie if I said I didn't look up Melissa Davis a few times online, but I could never find her."

Because she changed her last name, I thought. This is exactly why Jessica needs to see that letter and talk to Melissa.

"The box has meant a lot to me for many reasons and not just because it introduced me to the sweet tunes of New Kids on the Block."

Jessica laughs.

I glance at Lucas. "It also is the reason I got to meet Lucas, my first friend here. He's helped me with the box and finding you. There was a time I wanted to give up, but he wouldn't let me. He believed in me. And I'm so grateful to have him in my life."

Lucas gives me the biggest smile.

"Even though he can be a total nerd," I finish so his head doesn't get too big. "And I won't give up on this. It's important for you to know the truth. There was something added to the box that you have to see. It will give you some answers that I think would make you feel better. All we're asking is for you to allow us to come and deliver it to you."

There's silence on the other end.

I don't want to push her, but I think if situations were reversed and Lily had simply vanished from my life, I'd want to know why.

Jessica finally replies, and I do my best to remain calm.

"Okay, I'm going to have you talk to Ms. Ryan," I say in an even voice. "Nice speaking with you, Jessica."

I pass the phone to Lucas's mom.

"So?" Lucas looks at me expectantly.

I pump my fist in the air like I do when I kick a goal. "Are you ready for a road trip?"

CHAPTER TWENTY-FOUR

"You want to do *what*?"

So I guess there's one more obstacle I need to face.

Mom motions toward Dad accusingly. "Did you know anything about this?"

Dad holds his hands out—the spaghetti sauce on his fork dripping onto the kitchen table. "I knew she found a cassette tape, and I told you about that, but I didn't know that there was some box and that she and Lucas had—"

"Been going around behind our backs!" Mom's voice is getting high. "And now you want to drive four hours to some woman's house to give them a box? And you've been going around talking to strangers and getting into who knows what in a new town. Tell me, exactly, young lady, what on earth were you thinking?"

Honestly, I wasn't thinking she was going to react like this.

Okay, so yes, I probably, maybe should've told them more

about what Lucas and I were up to and probably, maybe shouldn't have just casually asked about going on this road trip in the middle of dinner.

Jackson's head is down as he types into his phone. I don't blame him for wanting to not be part of this discussion.

Although is it really a discussion when one side is doing all of the yelling?

"Peyton?" Mom stands up and taps her foot impatiently. "Please answer me."

There's silence in the room as everybody is waiting for me to say something.

"Where would you like me to start?" I begin. "Would you like me to start with the fact that you forced this move on the entire family? How you told us that everything was going to be *just great*? How we see less of you now that we're here? How—"

Mom cuts me off. "That's enough."

"Let her talk, Shannon," Dad says as he motions her to sit down. "You asked Peyton to explain, and that's what she's doing."

Mom exhales loudly as she sinks down in her chair.

"We're never together as a family," I say. "This is only our third meal we've had together since we moved. So, yeah, I did things and didn't tell you, but you never even asked. It was like as long as I was out of your hair it was fine. It wasn't a problem back home because I was usually busy with my friends. Well, they're not here. So I found a box and wanted to discover more about it. I'm sorry I didn't tell you, but it's not like I've had a lot of opportunity."

I feel lighter finally coming clean to my family about my frustrations.

"It's less than three and a half hours without traffic," Jackson throws out into the silence.

"What?" Mom asks him.

He holds up his phone, showing a map. "Hudson, Wisconsin—it's a little over thirty minutes east of Minneapolis, so it's a lot closer than our old apartment."

"That's not really the issue," Mom says as she pinches the bridge of her nose.

"But Peyton has a point," Jackson says. "Like, I know I'm on my phone and playing online and stuff, but, like, maybe we should have more family time. Isn't that what being in a smaller town is about? A simpler life?"

With that Jackson actually puts his phone, facedown, on the table.

Dad looks at the phone in his hand and does the same.

Jackson continues, "Peyton knows Lake Springs better than any of us. We even went out for lunch at Mimi's Café yesterday."

"You what?"

The fact that Jackson and I chose to go out in public together seems to have surprised Mom the most.

"How much of this town have you seen, Mom?" Jackson asks.

She opens her mouth and then closes it.

"So, like, why don't we have actual family time now that we're moved in?" Jackson blows out a breath, and his bangs move around. "Because if we had more moments like that, then it would be a lot harder for Peyton to think she can run around like Nancy Drew or something."

I shoot Jackson a look because that's so not what I was doing, but I do appreciate him sticking up for me.

"I'm sorry I didn't tell you what was going on," I say. I look over at Jackson, who gives me a supportive nod. "And that I haven't been very fair to you, Mom, because I know that this move has been hard on you as well. All I want is for us to start being a family again."

Mom gives me an appreciative smile. "That's all I want, too. And I will be around a lot more. Promise."

It's a start.

"I'm more than happy to tell you all about Lucas and what we discovered about these two girls who lived here in 1989. Melissa and I shared a bedroom."

"Oh!" Something registers on Mom's face. "That's why you were asking Dean Gibson about the house and how you knew about New Kids on the Block."

"Yeah."

"And of course you can go on this road trip," Dad says as

he pats me on the hand. "Maybe we should've been doing a better job about listening to you. So here we are. Your family, phones away, ready to hear what you have to say."

I talk and tell them everything. Not once does anybody reach for their phone.

We're finally starting to connect as a family.

CHAPTER TWENTY-FIVE

The original four-hour drive to Lake Springs at the beginning of the summer on this highway was miserable.

We were going to a place where I didn't know anybody. I was upset and scared.

This time the long drive is different.

There's excitement over what awaits us on the other side. We've been playing the mix I made from Melissa and Jessica's cassette tape.

Lucas's mom laughs as "Right Here Waiting" by Richard Marx comes on and Lucas and I sing along. Loudly and out of tune. "I can't believe you two know this song."

"It's, like, totally tubular," Lucas replies, which causes his mother to snort.

Like mother, like son.

"Yeah, gag me with a spoon!" I add.

So we may have looked up some sayings from the eighties. And might not entirely understand when to use them.

"We didn't all talk like that, you know," Ms. Ryan remarks.

"DON'T I!" Lucas and I scream in unison before cracking up.

Ms. Ryan shakes her head. "You two are too much."

Oh, we are.

Lucas and I have settled into a nice rhythm. Even though we might be done with the box, we're still making plans and hanging out. It's easy with him. He makes me laugh. He's teaching me cursive. I'm helping him with an old TV that he wants to repair. But most of all, he's made me feel more settled in my new home.

"What movie are we going to start with?" Lucas asks as he scrolls through the list of films from 1989 that we're going to watch when we get home.

We've become a little obsessed with that year.

"What are the choices?" his mom asks, her eyes fixed on the road.

Lucas begins reading them off his phone. "*Honey, I Shrunk the Kids*; *Indiana Jones and the Last Crusade*; *Look Who's Talking*; *When Harry Met Sally*—"

"Oh, that's one of my favorites," Ms. Ryan pipes in. "But I don't know if that's appropriate for you guys; it's a romantic—"

"Pass!" Lucas and I both reply.

"What else do you have?" I ask.

"*Turner and Hooch, Weekend at Bernie's, Parenthood, Bill and Ted's Excellent Adventure—*"

"Most excellent!" I say in the voice we found from a clip of the movie online.

"And then there are like a zillion sequels: *Ghostbusters II, Back to the Future Part II, Lethal Weapon 2* . . . We should probably watch the first movies before the sequels."

"Why don't we start with *Honey, I Shrunk the Kids* and go from there," his mom recommends. "That's more kid friendly."

"Rad!" Lucas replies.

"Stoked!" I add.

Lucas looks thoughtful for a moment. "Gnarly."

"You two do realize that Jessica isn't stuck in 1989, so maybe you can update your lingo to present day?"

"Don't have a cow, Mom!" Lucas says with a snort.

His mom shoots him a displeased look in the rearview mirror. "Oh, it doesn't matter what decade the language is from; there's no talking back, *dude*."

"Point taken, dearest mother," Lucas says with a smile on his face. "But really I think the most important question is, who is your favorite member of New Kids on the Block, Peyton?"

"I've been thinking a lot about this," I reply in a serious

tone. "As it seems like a pinnacle part of Melissa and Jessica's relationship."

"I think I'm a Danny guy; dude is buff." Lucas flexes his skinny arm.

"They all have their positive attributes, but I have to be Team Melissa on this one and go with Joey. Those eyes." I then throw my head back and pretend to swoon.

"He was my favorite, too," Lucas's mom adds.

The van slows down as we take the exit to Hudson.

We're almost there.

"That was a quick three and a half hours," Lucas says.

I was thinking the same thing.

There's silence in the car—save for Debbie Gibson telling us she's lost in our eyes—as we make our way to Jessica's.

We pull into a cul-de-sac and park in the driveway of a two-story house. There's a small ramp that's been put up to cover the steps to the front door.

"She insisted," Lucas's mom explains before Lucas can say anything about his mother making a fuss. "She's a doctor. She understands the importance of accessibility."

The front door is open, and a small child comes over to the screen. She's studying us as we get out of the van. She's about four years old with her hair in pigtails.

And then she appears.

Jessica stands behind her daughter. Her arms wrapped around herself. Her hair is short now. She's wearing glasses.

Instead of the bright neon dresses and shorts she wore as a kid, she's wearing gray leggings and a long black tunic. She gives us a hesitant smile.

"Hello!" Lucas's mom greets her as we make our way up to the porch. "Thank you so much for letting us come. This really means a lot to the kids."

"And I think it's going to mean something to you," I add. "Um, hi, I'm Peyton."

Jessica opens the front door. "Hi, Peyton and Lucas. Thanks for coming."

We enter the living room of her house.

"I'm Kylie!" the little girl says. "Do you like unicorns?" She runs over and grabs a stuffed unicorn.

"Hi, Kylie!" I reply. "And I do. They're the best!"

Kylie giggles in response as she hands the unicorn to Lucas, who waves it in the air like it's flying. "What's his name?"

"It's a *her*," Kylie says in an annoyed way that makes me instantly like her. "Beatrice!"

"Well, hello." A woman with dark brown skin walks into the living room. "I'm Jessica's wife, Leila." Leila scoops Kylie up in her arms. "We'll get out of your hair." She gives Jessica a kiss on the cheek.

"You have a lovely family," Lucas's mom says.

"Thanks. We have another on the way." Jessica goes over to a side table and shows us a picture of a little boy sitting up.

He has a cleft palate, a split on his upper lip. "We go to China next week so he can finally join our family. It's all Kylie can talk about."

"Congratulations," Lucas and I say at the same time and then look at each other.

"One, two, three, you owe each other a Coke," Jessica says with a wink.

"She owes me a lot of Cokes at this point," Lucas states dryly.

True.

"Why don't you make yourself comfortable?" Jessica gestures toward the couch. She has some fruit and vegetables out on the coffee table. "I thought you might be a little hungry after your drive. I forgot to ask about allergies, so I hope this is okay." She bites her lip.

"It's great," I reply, noticing that I'm not the only one who is a bit nervous.

I unzip my backpack and pull out the box.

Jessica gasps. "I can't believe it. I never thought I'd see that again."

I set it on the table next to her. Jessica looks at it like it's about to burst into flames.

She moves closer to it. Her finger traces the names. "I used to have such neat penmanship. Not so much anymore. I'm sorry to say that I've fallen into the stereotype of doctors having illegible handwriting."

She hesitantly opens the box.

A laugh erupts as she pulls out the New Kids on the Block collage. "Oh wow, this brings back memories. We were pretty obsessed."

"Were you, in fact, *hangin' tough*?" Lucas asks, his eyes sparkling with mischief since that was the name of one of their songs.

Jessica drops her head. "Oh my goodness. I can't believe you know that."

"We are well versed on 1989 knowledge now, and it's most excellent!" I proudly exclaim.

"Most excellent!" Lucas echoes me.

"And we also made our own mix from the one in the box," I add.

Jessica digs through and sees the tape. "Oh gosh, the mix. I remember how excited we were to make that. You were able to listen to this?"

"Yes, and we made a clean version." Lucas holds up the flash drive with the music. "We thought you might want to have this."

Jessica nods. "Yes, thank you. This is all so very . . . wonderful."

Her eyes light up. "Teddy!" She takes the small bear and hugs him. "She left him in the box for me. I thought . . ." She shakes the sadness that seems to be creeping up.

She goes through all the receipts. "We hated this movie,"

she says as she holds up the ticket stub for *Batman*. "We thought it would be fun. It ended up being really dark and weird. There were hardly any superhero movies back then, if you can believe that."

"I loved *Wonder Woman* and *Captain Marvel*," I add.

Jessica smiles. "Me, too. I had to wait my entire life to see Wonder Woman on the big screen, and it was worth it. I love that my daughter is growing up in a world where she sees strong women in leading roles. There's still a lot of work to do on Asian representation, though."

Jessica goes through the photos quietly, and then her attention focuses on the last one. Of an eleven-year-old her in tears.

She frowns. "There were so many things I thought would happen that summer. Never did I imagine I'd lose my best friend. I was so upset. I had no idea what I did wrong."

"You didn't do anything," Lucas says.

"I think you need to see the letter," I add.

Jessica takes the folded-up piece of paper and opens it up. The best friend necklace falls out. "Oh." Her bottom lip quivers. "This is in a special code we had. I think I can remember it."

"We already decoded it," Lucas says as he hands her the printout from his computer.

Jessica scans the letter. Her mouth drops open in shock. Tears fill her eyes. "I didn't know." She puts her head in her hands. "I had no idea it was that bad. I was too young to understand. I wish I would've known. Maybe I could've done something to help. How could she not say anything to me?"

I stand up. "You can still talk to her."

"What?" Jessica says. "You found Mel?"

Lucas holds out his phone. "Yes, and she knows we're here talking to you. She's just a touch of a button away."

Jessica smooths out her hair. "Oh, I don't know."

I think about Melissa who is at home hoping for a video call. I was that person at the start of the summer, waiting on Lily.

It's not a good feeling.

"Thirty years is such a long time, but . . ." Jessica holds out her hand to take Lucas's phone. "Better late than never."

With a shaking hand, Jess presses the video button.

Nobody moves or breathes as we wait for Melissa to pick up.

The screen fills with a woman with wavy, collar-length brown hair. "Jess!"

"Mel!" Jessica covers her mouth with her free hand. "I can't believe it."

"I'm so sorry—" Melissa begins.

"No, I'm sorry. I didn't know."

"I sent you a postcard."

Jessica looks confused. "When? I never got it."

"Oh, I don't know, maybe a month after we left. I put it in

our code because I was too worried someone would figure out it was from me. I didn't even put your name on it."

Jessica is stunned. "I wonder if my parents threw it out."

No. If only Jessica had gotten that postcard.

Melissa grimaces. "I was hoping you'd be checking the mail."

"Yeah . . . I stopped checking for a word from you after a couple weeks of silence."

Both women look heartbroken.

"Mama!" Kylie comes barreling into the living room with Leila chasing her from behind.

"Sorry," Leila replies as she picks Kylie up. "She's getting faster than me, which is scary."

"Is that your daughter?" Melissa asks.

Jessica makes introductions, and we watch these two best friends reconnect.

"I can't wait until you meet my son, Jesse," Melissa says.

Jessica looks stunned. "You remembered."

Melissa smiles. "I could never forget you."

Lucas's mom stands up and motions us to the door. "I think we need to give them some privacy. But you two did a really amazing thing, and I'm so very proud."

"But she has my phone," Lucas begins, but his mom shoos him out the door.

"We're just going to wait outside," she whispers to Jessica.

We sit outside on the front porch. Leila brings us some

lemonade and sandwiches as we wait for Jessica and Melissa to end their conversation.

Occasionally some laughter and delightful squeals drift over to us. I think it's going to be awhile.

"So now what?" I ask Lucas.

He lifts his eyebrow at me. "I have an idea. Scratch that, I have THE BEST idea."

CHAPTER TWENTY-SIX

ONE MONTH LATER

"Oh, come on! You can't be serious," I protest.

Lucas puts a flash drive on the kitchen counter in my house.

We ended up getting our own ramp for our front steps so Lucas can come over. Jessica was right: accessibility is important.

"I will not have that playlist be in my time capsule!"

"First of all, it's *our* time capsule," Lucas reminds me. "And you're more than welcome to do your own playlist, and we can have a more intelligent species be the judge."

"Which I will win," I reply confidently.

Lucas rolls his eyes. "Yeah, okay, sure. I guess we'll never know."

"Well . . ." I raise my eyebrows at him.

"Point taken," he says with a satisfied nod of his chin.

I finish braiding a friendship bracelet.

"I thought we already had the two we need for our box," Lucas says.

"Yeah, but I'm giving this one to Lily when I see her next week."

I reached out to Lily to have a real conversation. There were a few hurt feelings between us both, but not anything we couldn't get through.

If there's one thing I've learned from everything that happened (or didn't) between Melissa and Jessica it's this: don't let a friendship slip away. There will always be this distance between us, but she's still a very important part of my life.

In five days (yes, I'm counting), our parents are driving us to a meeting point halfway between our towns so we can spend time together. We already have a bunch of plans figured out, including hanging out with Callie. Then Lily's going to come here during the long weekend for Indigenous People's Day so she can meet Lucas.

We're not going to let the new people in our life take away from our friendship. They'll just add to it.

Plus, I hear Callie has a fierce flick pass that I want her to teach me.

"Meeting in person? How *retro*," Lucas adds with a wink.

We've been doing lots of retro things lately and having a pretty good time watching old movies and TV shows. The fashion alone is pretty hilarious. Big bright colors and poufy shoulders. Oh, and the bows. So many big bows.

Dad sticks his head into the living room. "Hey, P, for tonight do you want Sorry! or Life?"

"Life!"

"Nice! And Jackson is bringing a pint home, so we'll be properly prepared for board games and ice cream. Although, I didn't realize Jackson getting a job would make me need to work out more." Dad pats his stomach.

Yep, Jackson now leaves the house regularly to work at Frannie's. Mom and Dad even let me walk there all by myself, as well as to downtown and Lucas's house.

Who knew small-town living would mean more freedom? Well, once we got to know the place and people better. And I have my cell phone on at all times, and I send pictures and updates and . . .

But in a way, Mom being gone during the beginning of the move forced me to be more independent. I got to meet Lucas, discover the box and a lot more. Maybe my family is finally seeing me as the young lady they always say I'm becoming.

Dad turns to Lucas. "You staying for dinner, Lucas?"

"Wouldn't miss the Howard family screen-free Wednesday night activities for anything, Mr. H," Lucas replies.

"And free ice cream," I add.

"I mean, that's a given. And you all are invited to our screening of *Bill & Ted's Excellent Adventure* this weekend."

"Most excellent!"

Our families are also getting in on the retro fun. Lucas's family hosts 1989 movie nights while we have screen-free Wednesdays.

Both Lucas's phone and mine ping, and we cheer when we see that Jessica sent us a selfie of her and Melissa. They're having a long weekend reunion in Wisconsin Dells: Jessica, her wife, and now two children, and Melissa, her husband, and son. Then this September Melissa and Jessica are seeing New Kids on the Block in concert. They are *very* excited.

Lucas and I are tempted to join them, but it's a school night.

"Let's show them what we're doing," Lucas says as he sets up his camera on the counter to take a photo.

I stand next to him, holding a black shoebox with the Nike logo in silver on top. We've both signed the box in silver pens. I'm especially proud of my new signature, thanks to Lucas's lessons in cursive.

"You've inspired us," Lucas says as he types into his phone and sends them the picture.

Inside the box are items we collected this summer. Our own receipts from places we've gone to in Lake Springs—including Mimi's, of course—friendship bracelets, music, photos . . . We're still adding to it. We're going to bury it in my backyard before our first day of school, in the same place I found their time capsule.

It's fun to think about who will dig it up many years from now and what they'll think.

We do know that we're going to make it a lot easier to find us.

Then again, who knows where we'll be?

Our phones ping with a reply from Melissa. "Amazing!"

"YOU BOTH inspire us," Jess chimes in.

"You're THE BEST!" Melissa replies.

"THE BEST!" Jessica replies with a smiley face emoji.

Lucas beams at me. "Who would've thought when your dad made you do a gardening chore that it would lead us here?"

"No kidding, especially since I didn't know you even existed."

Lucas's expression turns serious. "What a dark, sad time for you," he says with a straight face before cracking himself up.

True.

When I picked up that shovel, I had no idea what would happen or where this summer would lead me. I was convinced it was going to be the worst summer ever, but in the end, it was sort of good. What with the mysterious box and reuniting two long-lost best friends and connecting with my family and everything.

Okay, okay. I'll admit it.

It's been the best summer ever.

ACKNOWLEDGMENTS

"Huh, what if I wrote about a girl who finds a time capsule?" Little did I know what journey that idea would take me on and the many, many people who would help me along the way. One could even say they were right here waiting for me. (Oh, if you don't know me by now, I'm totally going to find ways to drop 1989 song references throughout these acknowledgments. Girl, you know it's true.)

The majority of the first draft was written on a magical writing retreat powered by tzatziki. Thank you to Cassie Clare, Holly Black, Carrie Ryan, Marie Rutkoski, Josh Lewis, Maureen Johnson, and Kelly Link for answering questions, brainstorming, and not being driven *too* crazy when I'd start randomly singing throwback tunes. Let's just blame it on the rain.

To the wind beneath my wings, my agent Suzie Townsend for her support and coming up with THE BEST title. The entire New Leaf crew, especially Dani Segelbaum, is straight-up amazing. I'm so lucky to have you all on my team.

To my friends for the fun and nostalgic conversations about "then vs. now": Brigid Kemmerer, Tracy Shaw, Alvina Ling, Tara Coombs, Cathy Berner, and pretty much anybody I talked to for the entire spring and summer of 2019. I hold an eternal flame for Jen Calonita and Melanie Scales for reading an early draft of this book and giving me such wonderful feedback. And Jen, you're the only person with whom I'd be willing to share Joey.

I wanna have some fun, but I also want to do justice to my characters. Luckily, I can do both with T.J. Berardo! Thank you for your open conversations about being adopted from Korea and so much more. But this doesn't mean I'm going to go easy on you during *Quiplash*. Thanks also to Natali Cavanagh for your amazing and helpful notes.

You've got the right stuff, Abigail Johnson. I'm so indebted to your thoughtful comments regarding Lucas. And you've got, like, the best taste in boy bands (Abigail + Jonathan 4eva)!

Bloomsbury has been with me for every little step I take during this journey. Thank you to Erica Barmash, Faye Bi, Liz Byer, Jeffrey Curry, Phoebe Dyer, Beth Eller, Lex Higbee, Melissa Kavonic, Jeanette Levy, Cindy Loh, Donna Mark, Jasmine Miranda, Oona Patrick, Sarah Shumway, and Lily Yengle. Special shout-out to my editor Allison Moore for believing in this book from the earliest stages. Sorry for all!

The! Exclamations! But, like, Joey McIntyre IS so SWOONY!!!!! I get lost in his eyes.

Cover (girl) dreams do come true! I'm so fortunate to have a gorgeous cover thanks to Dana SanMar, who brought these characters to life. Upon seeing the cover, I sang, "She's got the look!"

Lake Springs is loosely based on my hometown of Portage, Wisconsin. During my electric youth, there were many, many trips to Book World, cheeseburgers eaten, and even more New Kids magazines purchased. Thank you to my family for not judging me *too* much (kidding, we know you did, *WJ*!). And, Mom, I'm sorry about all the tape marks you had to get sanded off my bedroom walls . . . and ceiling. To my Portage friends then and now—especially Amy, Kristi, and Autumn—for hangin' tough when I'm home (and letting me borrow your names). And *no duh*, I have to thank Joey, Jordan, Jonathan, Donnie, and Danny for helping me remember when.

To booksellers, librarians, educators, bloggers, readers—I'll be loving you forever. Your support over the years continues to astonish me. Now don't just stand there, bust a move!